MALCOLM
at
MIDNIGHT

BY
W. H. BECK

PICTURES BY
BRIAN LIES

HOUGHTON MIFFLIN BOOKS FOR CHILDREN
Houghton Mifflin Harcourt
BOSTON   NEW YORK

Houghton Mifflin Books for Children is an imprint of
Houghton Mifflin Harcourt Publishing Company.

www.hmhco.com

The text of this book is set in 11.45-pt. Palatino LT Standard.

The illustrations are pencil and powdered graphite on vellum.

Library of Congress Cataloging-in-Publication Data
Beck, W. H., 1970–
Malcolm at midnight / W. H. Beck ;
[illustrated by] Brian Lies.
p. cm.
Summary: Malcolm, a smaller than average rat, loves life at
McKenna School and the secret society of classroom pets that keep
children out of trouble, but when Aggy the iguana disappears Malcolm
must use all of his ratty persistence to prove his innocence and save her.
ISBN 978-0-547-68100-9 (hardback)
[1. Mystery and detective stories—Fiction. 2. Rats as pets—Fiction.
3. Pets—Fiction. 4. Animals—Fiction. 5. Schools—Fiction.
6. Secret societies—Fiction. 7. Humorous stories.] I. Title.
PZ7.B3812Mal 2012
[Fic]—dc23
2011048034

Manufactured in the United States of America
DOC 10
4500467279

FOR MY OWN NUTTERS
AND LANKY, CAL, ELI, AND DON.
—W.H.B.

TO MY SECOND GRADE TEACHER,
NANCY VANATTA—
A TEACHER OF VALOR
AND MERIT!
—B.L.

Dear Readers,

I found the following note and story on my desk
when I came in to work one morning. Who wrote it?
Well, I have my ideas . . .

Enjoy,

Mr. Mark Binney, fifth grade teacher

Dear Mr. Binney,

You asked us how that ring came to be on your desk the morning after the Dedication Day Carnival. You said we could leave you an anonymous note. That you just wanted — needed — to know. Well, it took a while, but here it is.

Some parts you may recognize. Some parts might get you mad. But all of it is true.

A lot happens in a school when the teachers aren't looking.

Sincerely,
Your Student

CHAPTER I
THE MOUSE

It began with a rat. There was also a glasses-wearing elderly iguana, a grumpy fish who could spell, a ghost in the clock tower, a secret message in the library, and a twisted evil that lived on the fourth floor of our school. But those'll all come later. First, there was a rat: Malcolm.

I know this'll surprise you, Mr. Binney, but yes, Malcolm's a rat. I know because he told me so.[1] Don't feel bad about bringing him to our class thinking he was a mouse. He *is* small. And that pimply clerk down at the Pet Emporium just wants to sell anything. I know—once he

---

[1] This'll come later, too. Just wait.

tried to convince me a goldfish was still alive even though it was floating upside down!

Remember, too—back then, last fall, you were kind of . . . distractible. Like a kid listening to his mom while Cartoon Network is blaring. Hearing, maybe, but not really listening. I know why now, but still. That must have helped the clerk's duplicity.[2]

So, I suppose, in an effort to get down the whole story, I should share how it happened. How Malcolm came to stay in Room 11 with us fifth-graders. I know you know

------

[2] Duplicity = dishonesty. Extra credit spelling/vocabulary word from Nov. 18's list. See? You thought our brains were like holey buckets, that nothing stayed in them. Not true. At least for most of us. Maybe it's true for Kiera.

this part, Mr. Binney, but I suppose it's important to tell the whole story.

Malcolm's story.

Malcolm doesn't remember much before the Pet Emporium. Maybe he was born there. He does know that he used to be in a cage with lots of other rats. But they all got sold. People want their money's worth, and the tiniest rat isn't the one to pick. Of course, when you're being sold as feeder rats, maybe that's not the worst thing.

So, Malcolm was the lone rat in his cage when you walked in that day, Mr. Binney. You came in for fish food, but somehow you found yourself stopped in front of the "Pocket Pets" section, jiggling a little square box in your hands. Every few minutes, you cracked it open and peeked inside.

Malcolm was racing on his wheel. He's very fast. Maybe you weren't really looking at him, but you have to admit, there's something about Malcolm that catches the eye.

The pimply-faced clerk noticed your pause. "Can I help you?" he asked. "Hey, don't you teach at McKenna School? I used to go there."

You jerked a little, snapped the box shut, and shoved it in your pocket. "Um—what? Yes, yes, I do." You pointed at Malcolm. "Cute . . . mouse. That brown splotch on his back almost makes him look like he's wearing a cape."

"Mouse?" The clerk frowned and chomped on his gum.

He glanced at the cage, then the frown switched to a slick smile. He slid in front of the sign that read RATS, $2.99 EACH and rolled his gum to the other side of his mouth. "Yes, he is a handsome one. You know, ra—*mice* make great classroom pets. And they're quiet and don't take up much room. Smart, too."

You both watched as Malcolm started licking himself. *All* over.

The clerk cleared his throat. "And, well—clean."

Malcolm finished grooming his tail. He considered your conversation. Whatever a "classroom" was probably was preferable to being sold to the next python owner.

Malcolm put his paws up on his food dish and stared at you. You've maybe never noticed, Mr. Binney, but Malcolm's got very intelligent eyes. Shiny dark brown, like steaming coffee. He added a little squeak.

You nodded. "Yes. Maybe. What kinds of supplies would I need?"

The clerk cracked his gum and grinned. "Well, let me show you our selection of cages and water bottles over here . . ."

And that was how Malcolm came to live in Room 11 at McKenna Elementary School in Clearwater, Wisconsin. With a three-story deluxe cage, a fleece-lined Comf-E-Cube, a tail-safe plastic exercise wheel, and a drip-free, antibacterial water bottle.

By the way, Malcolm wants to thank you for all that.

CHAPTER 2
McKENNA AT MIDNIGHT

Malcolm thought McKenna School might be the grandest place ever. Once at the Pet Emporium, he overheard a girl wearing a tiara describe a princess's castle. The steep brick walls, the rows of tall windows with their rippling glass, the tile and woodwork worn dark and smooth—it all seemed to fit. McKenna even had a tower with a white round face looming above the arched entrance. Of course, Malcolm's view of Clearwater up until then was the inside of a musty pet store and a rumbly Toyota, so anything was impressive. But still. He couldn't believe this was his home now.

That first day in Room 11 started with a bunch of sticky, sweaty kids all goggling at him and tapping his cage. Malcolm knew *this* from the Pet Emporium. He even recognized a few faces. And he knew what they wanted. Malcolm tossed shredded paper about. He spun his wheel. He raced through a toilet paper tube. The kids ooh'ed and ah'ed and giggled like they should. Even better, one tossed in a pinch of a Pop-Tart. Oh, it was heavenly. The food was certainly better at McKenna than those sawdusty pellets at the Pet Emporium.

The rest of that first morning was a blur of handing out books, labeling folders, and finding lockers. The room was packed with kids. It reminded Malcolm of the rat cage at the Pet Emporium when a new shipment of rats arrived. Lots of crowding, pushing, and squabbling as each kid staked out his territory. The classroom was so crammed with students that one, Amelia Vang, had to share Malcolm's table. Malcolm liked her right away. She lined up her notebooks and erasers just so. And each notebook was labeled. *Science. Math. Writing.* Malcolm wasn't sure what those things were, but he liked the order of it.

Finally, when Malcolm's head ached and buzzed from all the directions and rules, you pulled out your high stool, Mr. Binney, and opened a book. In fact, you pulled your stool right up next to Malcolm's cage. "Many of you have noticed our classroom pet. In honor of Malcolm, I have a special book for our first read-aloud: *The Tale of Despereaux.*"

Malcolm's ears perked up. How exciting to have a story read in his honor!

Then you continued, Mr. Binney. "It's a story with a mouse hero."

Malcolm's ears drooped. A *mouse* story? Hold on a whisker. Malcolm was willing to be mistaken for a mouse in order to not be sold as a snack for a snake, but this misunderstanding had to end! One thing people don't know about is that rats have a very strong sense of pride.

Then you started reading, Mr. Binney. Amelia had a copy of the book, too. While the rest of us were swept away within a few pages, a horrible feeling started to climb in Malcolm's stomach. He scanned ahead, trying to see the words on Amelia's pages. Was that what people really thought of rats? That they are sneaky, conniving, lazy, greedy? Malcolm retreated to his Comf-E-Cube and stuck his ears in the fleece.

That night, Malcolm lay awake in his cage. Rats are nocturnal,[3] so it wasn't unnatural for him to be awake in the dark. But this was different. You see, it was the first time Malcolm had ever—ever—been alone.

Can you imagine what it felt like for him to be alone for the first time? No hulking rats sitting on his face, no parrots across the room talking in their sleep, no wild mice sneaking in to get free meals from spilled kibble on the

---

[3] One way rats are superior to mice.

7

floor. Malcolm was alone. Shivery, echo-y alone. It was a wonderful and terrifying feeling. Finally, he got up to run a little on his tail-safe exercise wheel.

When you're alone, you have time to think. Malcolm's head was buzzing about how everyone at his new home thought he was a mouse. And that if they knew he was really a rat, they probably would be disgusted, and maybe even a little scared. Malcolm wondered what he could do about that.

When you're alone, you hear things you wouldn't normally hear. As Malcolm thought, he listened to the strange night sounds of McKenna. Far-off beeps and clicks. The distant thud of a door shutting. A faraway screech that made Malcolm shiver. Then the small creaks and cracks of the building settling.

When you're alone, you also notice things. Like the latch of the cage door. Malcolm slowed on his wheel. The wheel rocked back and forth as he stepped off it.

His door wasn't all the way shut.

Malcolm blinked. If he pushed hard enough . . . He grunted as his feet slipped. Then he did it. His pink nose was out in open air! Malcolm quickly wiggled the rest of his body through and leaped onto the counter.

Suddenly, the alone-ness, the thoughts, the sounds, they were all behind him. Now Malcolm trembled.

He was free.

Now, don't get me wrong. Malcolm was happy—

delighted—with life so far in Room 11,[4] but . . . well, if you noticed that something off-limits to you was suddenly not, wouldn't you check it out?

Maybe you'd answer differently, Mr. Binney. You're a teacher, after all. But I have to say that most regular folks—well, kids anyway (and rats, apparently)—would go for it.

Malcolm did. He figured he could easily squeak out and be right back. Surely you and the fifth-graders wouldn't return in the night. No one ever did at the Pet Emporium. Besides, he was hungry.

Malcolm's whiskers quivered. So many places to

---

[4] Except for the mouse-rat thing.

explore! He tiptoed over the neat stacks of papers and books. He took a drink from the sink. He wasn't really thirsty, but it tasted so much better than the water in his cage. Maybe it was all the bacteria.

He jumped down to the floor. Already, this was the farthest distance he had gone in his life. He had been born in a cage and lived in a cage. Malcolm sniffed out every corner of the room that night. Behind the bookcases. In the closet. Under the big desk up front. Down the marker rail of the white board. He even tried a little nibble of a social studies textbook, but it was too dry.

Then there it was: the door. It was shut, but a narrow slip of light at the bottom beckoned to Malcolm. A current of air blew in. Malcolm's nose twitched with exotic scents. Mud. Spoiled milk. Wet sneakers. He couldn't resist. He slipped under the door[5] and skittered down the edge of the hallway. It was dark except for a glowing sign at either end. As he traveled down the hall, Malcolm tried to memorize the school's layout. You may not know it, Mr. Binney, but rats have a remarkable sense of *feel*. It's all in their whiskers.

Malcolm followed his whiskers and nose to a long, cavernous room. Windows lined one side. The rest was full of rows of books. He recognized their scent because you have so many in your classroom, Mr. Binney.

---

[5] Some people think rats can compress their bones to fit through small spaces. They can't. But they are extremely flexible. Unlike mice.

At first, Malcolm wandered under the tables. He sniffed a pink eraser. He nibbled a stale cheese puff.

Then something caught his eye. A flash of silver from the long, low counter near the door. Malcolm scrambled up the desk chair, tiptoed across the computer keyboard, and came face-to-face with a glass cage filled to the top with swirling water.

An aquarium.

And deep in the dark water, shiny fish flashed their scales.

Malcolm, of course, was familiar with aquariums from the pet store. What's more, he had once seen a wild rat in the pet store go "fishing" for food with his tail. And here Malcolm was. All alone. Roaming free. For the first time.

Malcolm jumped up to the top of the aquarium. Along the back, open water churned. Malcolm peered into it, watching the shimmer of the fish. For a second he thought he spied something darker, something bigger, glide by. He blinked and leaned closer, but all he could see were the silver glints schooling near the top.

They were practically begging to be eaten.

Malcolm turned and stretched out his tail.[6] The fish scattered at first. Then they swam back over to investigate. One tasted the tip of Malcolm's tail. Malcolm stifled a giggle. It tickled!

_____

[6] You've probably never noticed, but if you looked at Malcolm's tail, you'd know in an instant he was a rat and not a mouse. Rats' tails are much more magnificent.

A bolder fish took a bigger bite. This was it! Malcolm pulled his tail up fast, but the fish slipped off and fell back in. Nubbins! This was trickier than it looked.

Malcolm was about to try again when suddenly they scattered like spitballs out of a shooter. Before Malcolm could register what was happening, a dark shape burst from the water's surface. A giant mouth opened. Then it closed—with Malcolm's tail caught inside.

Yow! You remember how much Jovahn whined when he stuck his finger in the electric pencil sharpener, Mr. Binney?[7] Well, this was every bit as painful. More, maybe. Malcolm squealed and shot straight up.

But the grip on his tender tail wasn't Malcolm's only problem. No, whatever was attached to that mouth wasn't letting go. In fact—Malcolm started fumbling furiously at the edge of the glass—it was pulling him into the water.

Malcolm scrabbled for a pawhold. His claws left tiny

---

[7] You should see all the stupid stunts Jovahn pulls when you're out of the room.

grooves in the hard black plastic of the aquarium's lid as they scraped across its surface. But little by little, Malcolm was dragged into the swirling water.

Splash! Malcolm's back legs fell in. He rat-paddled furiously. Gristle, he was a goner! How could this be happening?

Then his back right toes caught hold of the edge of the lid. With this new grip, Malcolm heaved himself back toward safety. Whatever held his tail pulled back—at first. Then it didn't.

Like a rubber band shot across a classroom, Malcolm launched into the air. He flew over the aquarium and the edge of the counter. Then he was falling, falling. Finally, with a soggy thud, Malcolm landed on the worn carpet of the library floor.

Oof. Malcolm's shoulder ached, he was half-soaked, and his tail throbbed. He looked up at the aquarium. Only the sloshing water at the top gave any indication of the struggle he'd been through. What *was* that thing in there?

And then—*brrrrring!*

A bell jangled through the silence. It was a long, drawn-out rattling sound that seemed to go on and on. Malcolm's whole brain vibrated with the noise. He squeaked and leaped up so quickly, he smacked his head on a table leg. The noise came from a glass and metal disk that hung over the door. Two black arrows on it pointed straight up.

Malcolm didn't know about clocks or time yet, but it was exactly midnight.

In the quiet after the bell stopped, the noises really started. First a *thump, thump, thump*—getting louder as it came closer. Then a *pitter-pat, pitter-pat.* And then—most terrifying of all—a slow and steady *scritch . . . scritch . . . scritch.*

Malcolm trembled and darted around. Where to hide? Where to hide?

Thump, thump, thump.

Pitter-pat, pitter-pat.

Scritch . . . scritch . . . scritch.

They were headed his way.

CHAPTER 3
THE MIDNIGHT ACADEMY

Malcolm backed away from the noises in the hallway. His sore tail hit a bookcase and he squeaked in pain. But he didn't have time to think about that. Whatever was making those noises had entered the library. The sounds were more muffled now, but still growing closer. Malcolm scurried up two shelves.

He ducked behind a row of thick *Harry Potters*. *Crinkle*—what was *that?* An old Cheezy Bit Snack Cracker bag, tucked behind the books. Malcolm pushed it away. He pulled a whisker into his mouth and nibbled nervously. Should he look? Malcolm peeked around the corner of the books.

And his mouth fell open.

At the front counter of the library, a blue glow lit up the room. It was the computer. Someone had flipped it on.

Someone with green scales and a long tail. An iguana.

And there wasn't only an iguana. It was like being at the pet store all over again, only no cages and no pimply clerk with his pizza-smelling hands. Malcolm stared. There was a tarantula, a white, silky lop-eared rabbit, two hamsters, a hermit crab, a hedgehog, a box turtle, a parakeet, and three baby chicks.[8]

The iguana at the computer lowered her face and pushed it along the desk. When she raised her head, red reading glasses balanced on her nose, the sides crisscrossed at the back of her spiky neck.[9] Her orange eyes looked as big as bouncy balls behind the lenses.

The iguana rapped her long claws against the countertop. "Now, now. Let's get started. The bell has rung after all." The rest of the animals crawled, hopped, climbed, and skittered up to the countertop next to her. The chicks had to get a little boost from the rabbit.

"Does anyone have any announcements?" the iguana asked. She peered over her glasses. She cleared her throat. "I said, does anyone have any announcements? Because if not, we really have a very full agenda tonight. The hand sanitizer is missing from all the second grade classrooms. It's a very peculiar theft. And one not likely committed by the second-graders. They never wash on purpose.

---

[8] You probably recognize these pets from the classrooms around you, Mr. Binney. You might also have a hard time believing the next bit. But stay with me.

[9] I'm not sure we need to mention to Mrs. Snyder that her glasses are worn by a lizard at night. She has enough to worry about with overdue books.

Furthermore, there have been some rumblings from our district informants about possibly banning classroom pets again this year. And, there's been a sighting. Snip's been on the move up on the Fourth—what's that, Honey Bunny?"

The rabbit cleared her throat. She had the shiniest coat Malcolm had ever seen. Silky white fur, long, drooping ears, and deep, liquid eyes. Probably cost a fortune at the pet store.

She opened her delicate mouth and, in a deep, gravelly voice, said, "Looks like Oscar there has something he wants to say."

Malcolm blinked. Guess the rabbit was a *he*.

"Oh, yes. Oscar." All eyes turned to the aquarium. One of the hamsters ran up to the top and clicked on a light, saying, "Sorry. Sorry! We didn't forget about you."

Malcolm's eyes bugged. *That* was what bit him? Inside was a monstrous fish—orange and black and as big as Jovahn's sneaker. Malcolm's tail throbbed seeing the fish. His tail! His lovely rat tail was now a limp, frazzled mess, red and painful at the tip where that *beast* had chomped him.

"Yes, we're sorry, Oscar," said the other hamster. The fish turned its back to the group.

"Oh teeth and claws," grunted the rabbit. "Who needs Mr. Moody over there? Come on, I've got some fresh banana chips to get back to."

The fish—Oscar—streaked across the water, sending a

splash over the edge and drenching the hamster and hedge-hog. The hedgehog spluttered. And the chicks peeped like mad.

Then the fish started nosing at the gravel in his aquar-ium. Pushing and piling it this way and that. The other animals drew closer, until Malcolm couldn't see from his shelf. But he could hear them.

"Yes, yes." "What?" "Oh, *really* . . ."

Suddenly the group of animals turned and scanned the bookcases. Malcolm ducked behind the *Harry Potter*s just in time. He nibbled furiously on the whisker in his mouth.

"Behind F Row, Oscar?" the iguana asked. Malcolm heard her slide off the counter.

"Careful, Aggy," warned the turtle. "Could be a wild one."

"Oh, I don't think so. I heard Ms. Brumble mention something." The iguana's tongue flicked in and out with a quiet hissing sound. "Besides, smells like snack crack-ers up here."

"Well, that could be any of the nutters around this place."

"No, there's something . . ."

Things grew quiet. Malcolm trembled behind the books. What was going on out there? In the silence and the dark he couldn't tell. Gristle, why had he ever left his cage? Right now he could be sucking on his bacteria-free water and dozing in his Comf-E-Cube. What had he been thinking—exploring, leaving his cage? He was a pet rat, for scrap's sake! He didn't belong out here.

Then—there it was again. *Scritch, scritch, scritch.* Closer—and closer. Malcolm's whiskers twitched. His ears swiveled. His rat nose should be picking up something. But all he could smell were Cheezy Bits. He wanted to run, but where? He was caught as surely as Kiera had been caught with Tianna's note earlier in the day.

He waited. Silence. Then—*scritch, scritch.*

That was it. Malcolm couldn't stand it. He poked his head out of the shelf.

If rats could scream, he would have. As it was, he made a high-pitched squeak that sounded very undignified. Peering around the books at him was the iguana with her giant red reading glasses.

She opened her mouth. Malcolm flinched. He didn't remember if iguanas were carnivorous, but even so, that didn't mean she didn't have some venom or something. A long tongue flicked for a minute. The orange bouncy-ball eyes ran down the length of Malcolm's small, quivering body, stopping briefly on the tip of his tail.

Then she said, "Aren't you coming?"

Malcolm looked up at the lizard. "C-coming?" he managed.

The iguana nodded. The glasses slid down her snout a little. "To join us, of course. The Midnight Academy."

CHAPTER 4
THE KNACK

Malcolm shot a glance at the aquarium. "Join you?" The orange and black fish seemed to be smirking at him.

The iguana nodded slowly. "Well, yes. Preferably over on the counter. Though I suppose we could all come up here. But we really do depend on the computer to take our notes. It's hard for most of us, holding a pencil. Octavius can type much faster." Malcolm glanced at the computer and saw the tarantula poised on the keyboard.

"Computer?" Nubbins, he sounded ridiculous repeating everything she said. But his tail throbbed, and he was talking to a glasses-wearing lizard! That would make it hard for anyone to think.

Malcolm didn't really have a choice, anyway. He followed the iguana down the bookshelf and back up to the library's counter and the glow of the computer.

Once he was there, the other animals backed away from him and stood in a half circle. Malcolm felt smaller than ever. He held his aching tail in his front paws and tried to stand up straight.

The iguana smiled.[10] "There now. So. I'm Aggy Pop. And this," she gestured at the scowling rabbit, "is Honey Bunny. These hamsters are Jesse James and Jesse's good sister, Billy the Kid; Pete's the hermit—crab, that is; here's Harriet Beecher Stowe, the hedgehog; Octavius I've already mentioned; our three chicks, Polly the parakeet, and that's Tank the Turtle. Of course, you've already met Oscar the Grouch." A little splash plunked out of the top of the aquarium. "Don't mind him. But don't put anything in his aquarium, either. Today's Thursday. All three kindergarten classes visit the library on Thursdays. He has to put up with a lot. It would wear on anyone."

Malcolm nodded dumbly and covered the sore tip of his tail. He glanced at the bottom of the tank. Mixed in the gravel were beads of different colors. As Malcolm watched, the fish nudged the beads around in the gravel until "NICE TO MEAT YOU" was spelled out. The giant fish bared his teeth in a grin over the word "meat."

---

[10] Have you ever seen an iguana smile? It's not the most comforting thing to see. Especially if you are smaller than she is.

Malcolm sidled away from the tank. "Nice to meet you all, too."

"So what are you doing here, mouse? Spying on us?" said the gruff voice of the rabbit.

Malcolm jumped. "Spying? What? I—I just came—I was . . . hungry." Malcolm winced. *Hungry?* Why did he say that?

Malcolm decided to start over. He stood taller and tried to ignore how short he had chewed two of his whiskers. "First of all, I'm Malcolm. And I'm not a—"

The rabbit interrupted. "Hold on—you're not a rat, are you?" He turned to Aggy and Oscar. "We can't have a rat. Not after what happened the last time. How do we know he's not a spy from the Fourth?"

The hedgehog sneezed. "Look at him, HB. A rat? A spy?" She sniffed. "He's a mouse, and not much of one. He'd never survive the Fourth. The moths alone would eat him."

Aggy banged her claws on the counter again. "Let's start over here. Let's call our meeting to order first. Malcolm, we'd like to welcome you to the Midnight Academy. It doesn't matter what you are."

Aggy looked meaningfully at the hedgehog. "Harriet?"

The hedgehog sighed. "The Midnight Academy. Our pledge is to keep the halls of McKenna School safe through thick and thin as only critters can do," she rattled off in a phlegm-soaked voice.

"Well, you could say it with a little more gusto, Harriet."

The hedgehog sneezed again. "I'm sorry. I may be allergic to mice as well as people."

Malcolm burst in. He didn't know where to start. "Actually, I'm—wait. The Midnight Academy? You're a—a" —he searched for the word he had heard some kids mention earlier that day—"a club?"

"A club?" Honey Bunny snorted. Oscar flipped in his aquarium. The chicks peeped, "Neep, greep, weep!" Even the tarantula crossed his first two legs and pressed them to his furry brow.

"A *club*?" Honey Bunny repeated. "Was it a *club* that exposed the natural gas leak at Roosevelt School? A *club* that alerted the media to the copy paper scandal? A *club* that helps to track down Michael Simmons each and every time he runs away from art class? I don't think so. And not only that, but we do it all seamlessly. With no lankies or nutters even knowing we're there. We're clean. In and out without a trace. We're not a Brownie troop, snacking on cookies. This is a serious organization with years of prestigious history, long before your great-great-great-granddad was even a ball of fluff." Honey Bunny turned to the group. "Are we sure we want to share with this runt? He doesn't seem fully appreciative."

Malcolm stuttered, "Well, wait. I—you mean you're a secret group that helps the school?"

"Not only helps the school," one of the hamsters— Malcolm thought it was Jesse James—said. "In many

27

ways, we *run* the school. The Midnight Academy is the ears, eyes, nose, and whiskers of the school. We've got critters in high places all over the district."

Billy the Kid continued. "The lankies don't know, of course, but that's only because that's the way we want it."

Malcolm felt like he would positively burst. A secret group that took care of the school? What an opportunity! But wait. "Lankies?" he asked.

Billy the Kid shrugged. "Lankies. You know, the people. Humans."

"Not to be confused with the nutters. Those are the little ones. The kids. Smell like peanut butter and act crazy most of the time?" Jesse James grinned, made a face, and did a back flip, like Malcolm had seen one of the kids[11]— nutters—do after recess the day before.

But Honey Bunny interrupted again. He turned to Aggy. "He's not respectful. And he's a, well, what are you? Mouse or skuzzy rat?"

Malcolm's throat grew dry. Not the critters, too! Did the whole world have a bad opinion about rats? But Aggy stepped forward before Malcolm could speak up. "Oh, hush, Honey Bunny. He's only learning of the Academy for the first time right now. What do you think, Malcolm? Joining us would be a very serious responsibility. One that might mean putting the school's needs over your own wants." Her orange eyes flicked to Malcolm's tail. In his

---

[11] I probably don't need to note that it was Skylar. But maybe you don't know that that was how Simon got his bloody nose.

excitement, he had let it drop. Now he scooped it up again and tucked it behind him. Gristle, had she seen him and Oscar before?

Despite this, Malcolm's heart fluttered. Yes, he was ready. Maybe he'd prove them all wrong about rats. He cleared his throat and said in his most dignified voice, "I'd love to join you."

Aggy's eyes crinkled at the corners. "Excellent," she said. "Octavius, please make a note of it." The tarantula gave her a salute and started typing. "Malcolm, you're our first pledge in quite a while. The chicks aren't full members yet, either, of course. But it's a little different with them. They need to grow up first."

"And learn how to talk in sentences," muttered Jesse James.

"Peep, cheep, deep!" One of the chicks fluttered at Jesse and he ducked.

Aggy ignored them. "Pledges aren't full members right away. There's a trial period. And a lot to learn about the organization. First, we meet every Thursday night, right here, after the night custodian goes home. Jesse will ring the all-clear bell. Do you need any assistance getting out of your cage?" She paused. "I suppose not; you're already here, aren't you? Well, then next are your intensive reading lessons. You aren't much use without that. We'll need to get you up to speed."

"Oh, lettuce wilt," Billy the Kid moaned. "He doesn't *read?*"

"Cheez, you sure you didn't come from the kindergarten rooms?" Jesse James added. The rest of the group groaned and buzzed.

Aggy drew her claws along the countertop. They made a long screeching sound that brought everyone back to order. "Of course he doesn't read. We all started out not reading, Billy. It might do you good to remember." Then she turned to Jesse. "And sometimes we learn a lot in the kindergarten rooms. Like manners."

"Reap heaps," The chicks peeped and agreed.

Aggy turned to Malcolm. "Now, now. Don't feel ashamed. Even our founding father, Thomas Jefferson, the guinea pig, didn't read at first. And look at all he did for the schools. I'll teach you myself. Meantime, for tonight, Honey Bunny will help you go over the handbook and rules. Harriet, would you fetch it?"

The hedgehog lumbered off with a sniff.

"Hold on." Honey Bunny flattened his ears. "*I'm* not taking on another pledge."

Tank snorted and muttered, "Let's hope not."

Honey Bunny glowered at him and the turtle yanked his head into his shell.

Aggy held up a clawed foot to interrupt. "Malcolm will be *my* pledge. Didn't I say I'd teach him? I thought you might take him to the back as a favor to me, HB. You already know the ins and outs of what's on the agenda tonight. And Malcolm, as a pledge, is not ready to hear it all quite yet."

Malcolm felt like the conversation was going too fast, like when Jenna reads aloud in class and it sounds like allthewordsaretypedtogetherwithoutanyspaces. Malcolm was still a few sentences back. "But—but—wait," he finally sputtered. He thought of Amelia and her notebooks. *Despereaux.* The exit signs, the Cheesy Bits Snack Cracker bag. "Reading's making sense of those shapes, isn't it?" He looked around at the group. "But they already do. Make sense, I mean. Look—" He hopped down the counter and pointed to a sign. "'Return books here.'"

His statement had the exact same effect as that one time Jovahn blabbed about the tooth fairy to the first-graders—remember, Mr. Binney? Octavius pressed a front leg over his fangs. Tank and Pete yanked their heads into their shells and peeked out. Jesse froze with Billy in a headlock. Even Honey Bunny's mouth was open.

Harriet the hedgehog dropped the notebook she was

31

carrying in her mouth and narrowed her eyes. "How long did you say you've been at McKenna School?"

Malcolm felt himself shrink. But surely, reading was a good thing. Didn't all the other animals—critters—say they could read, too? And you were always talking about how great it was in class, Mr. Binney. But how *had* Malcolm learned to read? He didn't remember. It was simply something he knew. "Since—since the—um, a day?"

Jesse James and Billy the Kid sucked in their breath at the same time.

"Well," Aggy said softly. "That's quite remarkable. You must have a Knack."

"A Knack?" Malcolm repeated.

"A special talent—something you're extra good at. Something to help you. Like how Jesse James and Billy the Kid can get into any room and Octavius can type two hundred words per minute. Reading's an unusual one because it's so complicated. Most humans take several years to learn to read. And you're telling us you've already learned it. In a day."

Honey Bunny, who had recovered himself, jerked his pink nose at Malcolm. "We'll see about that. Come on, follow me." He snatched up the slim notebook that Harriet had dropped and loped off to the back of the room. "Do your meeting, Aggy."

Malcolm edged away from the group and followed Honey Bunny's round fluffy behind. It really was a remarkably cute fluffy behind. But Malcolm bet that Honey

Bunny didn't want to hear that now. Behind him, the rest of the group was silent, waiting for the two to leave. Waiting to talk about Malcolm, probably.

Honey Bunny stopped under a table. He stretched out his front paws. He clicked on a small flashlight that was duct-taped to the underside of the table. He saw Malcolm staring. "First Academy rule: Be prepared. Yeah, we stole that from the Boys Scouts—the motto, not the light—well, actually, we probably stole the light from them, too. But, by claw, we've had to sit through enough of those meetings after school. We could all be Eagle Scouts by now. Might as well use some of their stuff."

Honey Bunny settled the notebook into the beam of light on the floor. "Okay, go."

Malcolm had never read out loud before. Much less in front of anyone. And Honey Bunny wasn't exactly a friendly audience. Malcolm felt like a cheese puff was stuck in his throat. He tried to swallow and made a loud gulping noise. "Being Critter-Wise: The B-b-bylaws of the Midnight Academy. One, never get caught out of your cage. Two, never communicate with humans. Three, report suspicious activity to each meeting..." Malcolm's voice faded. Honey Bunny was staring at him now. "Did I, did I, say it wrong?"

Honey Bunny glanced toward the light of the computer in the front of the library. Everyone up there was hunkered around Octavius. Then before Malcolm even knew what hit him, Honey Bunny slammed out his front legs and flipped Malcolm over on his back. Malcolm grunted as the wind shot out of him. Honey Bunny pinned Malcolm down with a heavy paw that smelled like fresh banana chips.

"Who are you really?" Honey Bunny hissed. "Are you working with Snip? You're a rat, really, aren't you?"

Malcolm wheezed, trying to suck air back into his lungs. "S-snip? What's that?"

Honey Bunny narrowed his rose-pink eyes and pressed harder.

Malcolm swallowed. Underneath that white, fluffy fur

was a rabbit of steel. Malcolm could barely take a breath. "I don't know what you're talking about. I'm a pet. I swear! A pet—" Honey Bunny shifted. Malcolm could feel a claw—a not-at-all-soft-and-fluffy claw—piercing the skin on his belly. Malcolm gasped. "I'm a pet—mouse!"

Up front, the computer light flickered. A twitter of laughter floated back from the front of the room. Honey Bunny glanced toward it and lifted his paw. Malcolm scrambled to his feet. Gristle, what was *that* all about?

"Well. That's amazing," Honey Bunny's voice boomed

out across the quiet library in fake joviality.[12] "Reading. After only one day of fifth grade. You'll make a remarkable addition to the Academy, *mouse*."

Malcolm blinked. Mouse. Not again. And worse, Honey Bunny didn't sound like he even believed Malcolm. But then, why did it matter so much to Honey Bunny what Malcolm was, anyway?

Honey Bunny stepped between Malcolm and the rest of the Academy, blocking their view. He jabbed Malcolm with that same sharp claw and muttered, "There are two last rules. Unwritten ones. First: Don't call me Honey Bunny. I tolerate it from Aggy, but no one else. Understood?"

Malcolm nodded.

"And two: You'd better be telling the truth. We don't like rats. They're skuzzy garbage-eaters who lie and cheat. Aggy may be all friendly, but she's not practical like the rest of us. There's not a rat on this planet that isn't out to help himself. I've seen it myself." He pawed at his silky ears. "We have a saying here in the Academy: 'A critter reveals his true self at midnight.' It means the way you are when no one is looking—that's the critter you really are." He jabbed one last time for emphasis. "But don't worry. *I'll* be looking. Oh yes, I'll be watching for your true self."

Malcolm gulped. He couldn't think of a thing to say.

Instead he followed Honey Bunny's cute, fluffy behind back up to the front of the library.

---

[12] Jovial = cheerful. Kiera was positively jovial when she and Tianna were paired up in science class. Vocabulary from 12/3.

CHAPTER 5
THE EARS, EYES, AND NOSE OF ROOM 11

Back in Room 11, Malcolm banged his head on the corner of his cage. A mouse? A *mouse*? How in the name of all specks, scraps, and morsels had those words come out of his mouth?

Now, not only did the fifth-graders think he was a mouse, but so did the critters. And this time it was his fault! Now what? How could he possibly fix it? How do you casually say, "Oh, I made a mistake. You know what? I'm really a whole different species." No, if Honey Bunny thought rats were "skuzzy garbage-eaters who lie and cheat," then admitting to a lie wasn't going to convince him otherwise.

Malcolm flopped on his back in his Comf-E-Cube and stared at the wire grid of his cage.

The ears, eyes, nose, and whiskers of the school.

Those words echoed in Malcolm's head. Despite the rat-mouse thing, Malcolm felt excitement and pride stir inside him, too. A secret group. And they wanted him to belong! Even at the Pet Emporium, Malcolm had always been left alone, left out. It's hard to make friends when they keep getting scooped up and sold as snake food.

Maybe the answer to his mouse problem was in the Academy itself. Malcolm remembered something you had said earlier that day, Mr. Binney. It was right after you set down *The Tale of Despereaux*. Remember? You talked to us about what kind of fifth-graders we wanted to be this year. How it was all in our choices, every minute of our days. How even grownups like you had to think about it sometimes, to be the person they wanted to be.

It reminded Malcolm about the Academy saying Honey Bunny had shared. "A critter reveals his true self at midnight." Malcolm knew that Honey Bunny had said it more as a threat, but it got Malcolm thinking. What if he could prove to the Academy that he was a critter of . . . of—what were some of the words you had used, Mr. Binney?— valor[13] and merit?[14] Maybe if he acted with valor and merit, he could admit the truth. Maybe then everyone could start thinking that not all rats are skuzzy.

Yes. Malcolm would be the best pledge the Academy

---

[13] Valor = heroic courage. Mr. Binney shows valor in choosing to teach fifth-graders year after year. Vocabulary from 9/2.

[14] Merit = worthy of praise. Jovahn's ability to burp the alphabet is of merit, if you are impressed with such things. Also from 9/2.

had ever had. Starting in the morning, Malcolm would be the ears, eyes, nose, and whiskers of Room 11. He'd have something to bring to the Academy meeting next Thursday. Something that would wilt the whiskers off that Honey Bunny.

For the next week, Malcolm watched the kids—*nutters*—in the classroom. And as the days passed, patterns emerged. Mornings were quiet—just you, Mr. Binney, shuffling papers and peeking in the little square box that you had that first day at the Pet Emporium. Malcolm could see it better now and could tell it was a deep blue and covered in some kind of fuzzy cloth. Then the bell would sound, you'd snap the box shut, and the room would fill with the bustle of thirty fifth-graders pushing inside at once, their faces flushed and smelling of fresh air and Cheerios.

Days aren't Malcolm's active time, so he marveled at all the energy behind the sights and sounds and smells of the room. The variety of giggles, sighs, sniffles, coughs, sneezes, and burps. How loudly Skylar shouted out answers. The rumble and scrape of the chairs as the nutters leaped up to leave for lunch every day. The whiffs of peanut butter, sweat,[15] eraser dust, dry-erase markers, and strawberry shampoo.[16]

---

[15] Especially after recess and from Jovahn.

[16] That was Amelia Vang's.

During this time, Malcolm especially observed Amelia Vang. How could he help it? She was literally right under his stubby whiskers.[17] While Malcolm admired Amelia's sense of order—her hair elastic matched her socks every day!—what he liked best was how Amelia talked.

"How are you doing, Malcolm?" she murmured to him every morning. And Malcolm would squeak back and bask in the smile she flashed at him. Amelia talked to Malcolm like he was already a critter of valor and merit.

Malcolm's favorite part of the day was at the end, when the class took turns meeting with you in groups, Mr. Binney, at the front table for reading. When it wasn't Amelia's turn to go up front, Malcolm had her all to himself. She would talk and he would listen.

I'm sorry to say, Mr. Binney, that sometimes during afternoon reading groups, the rest of the class isn't always acting like the fifth-graders you want them to be. Sometimes they're goofing around. Nothing obvious, but a lot of whispers, doodles, and gum.

That Thursday afternoon, during this time, Jovahn fiddled with a slingshot he had made out of a plastic spoon and rubber bands. Kiera frowned at him as she plastered her mouth with lip gloss (wild mountain berry-berry) and passed notes to Tianna. Malcolm half listened to the buzz of the classroom as he dozed in his Comf-E-Cube.

---

[17] Malcolm vowed he would grow them out—so he could better serve the Academy. But gristle, it was hard!

Then a Jovahn-launched paper clip zoomed off course and flew through the wire of Malcolm's cage. It bounced off Malcolm's nose. He yelped in surprise at the sting.

"You hurt him, you big lummox!" Amelia scolded. She unlatched the door and reached into Malcolm's cage.

Jovahn whispered back, "Well, I wasn't trying to! I was trying to—never mind." Jovahn glanced at you, Mr. Binney, still busy with a reading group at the front table. He crept back to Amelia's table. "Is he okay?"

Amelia scooped Malcolm out of the cage and cradled him against her chest. "Yes. No thanks to you." She stroked her finger down his back.

Malcolm nearly swooned with the warmth and softness of Amelia's sweater. This was the first time Malcolm had ever been picked up and held and petted. Before, it had only been a quick scoot and shove as his cage had been cleaned at the Pet Emporium. And you, Mr. Binney, while providing a warm, safe, luxurious home, hadn't exactly taken to cuddling with Malcolm.[18] Imagine going your whole life never being touched gently!

Kiera raised her hand then. "Mr. Binney, Jovahn's out of his seat again."

You looked up, Mr. Binney. And you sighed and rumpled your hair. It stuck up a little in the back, but you

---

[18] Malcolm suspects it was Amelia's tender touch that clouded his judgment and caused him to do what he did next. It's not an excuse for it, mind you. Just a reason.

didn't notice.[19] "Back to work, Jovahn. Kiera, take care of yourself, please."

Jovahn slunk away. "Rat fink," he muttered under his breath as he passed Kiera's desk. She sniffed and slicked on some more lip gloss.

Rat fink? Malcolm stiffened against Amelia's sweater front. What did *that* mean? Nothing good, from Jovahn's tone. The words hit hard, like Honey Bunny's paws on the first night of the Academy.

Amelia felt the change in Malcolm. She set him down on her notebook. She leaned over and pulled out her hair elastic. Her long, dark hair made a perfect strawberry-scented curtain, shielding Malcolm from the rest of the class. "What's wrong, mousie? Don't let that neanderthal bother you."

Mousie. Rat fink. Malcolm wobbled. It was a double blow. Yes, Amelia talked to him like a critter of valor and merit. But not as a rat. She had been talking to him as a mouse.

At this same time, Malcolm's stubby whiskers twitched at the texture of the smooth paper under him, and the inky smell of Amelia's writing. That morning, after reading *The Tale of Despereaux*, you had asked the class to write a note about what they liked and didn't like about the story so

---

[19] Kiera says she can judge your mood by how much your hair sticks up in the back, Mr. Binney. The spikier the hair, the grumpier the mood. I hate to say it, but she may have something there.

far.[20] Amelia's notebook was still open to her paragraph. The words curled underneath Malcolm's paws like a delicate garden of flowers.

Hold on a whisker. Malcolm tiptoed around the page. The words. His Knack. Hadn't Aggy said that each animal has a Knack to help them? Here was his. No more "mousie." No more "rat fink." The *words*—they were right under him. Did he dare?

Before Malcolm could think any more about it, he hopped to the top of the page. "Hey," Amelia cried, but not too loudly. "Malcolm, get back here!"

But Malcolm wasn't going far. He tapped his hind foot on a word in the first sentence, "not."

Amelia tried to pick him up. Malcolm dodged her and stomped harder above the word. He squeaked, and he pointed with his front paw. Then he pointed with the tip of his tail (which was still sore from Oscar the Grouch).

Amelia's brow furrowed. "What? What's got you so excited? You're going to get us in trouble." She reached in her bag and came out with a chunk of graham cracker. She held it out to Malcolm. "Come on. Back to your cage."

Malcolm's head swam. It was a cinnamon-sugar graham, his favorite. But "mousie" rang through his head. He uttered another squeak and thumped his foot on the word.

---

[20] Believe me, never before had Malcolm so wished he could write. He'd have a lot to say about that story if he could.

Amelia slowly set down the graham cracker. "What is it?"

Malcolm tapped on the page. He ran the tip of his tail along the bottom of the word, like he had seen you do, Mr. Binney, with Skylar's reading group, when you are trying to get them to sound something out.

Something flickered in Amelia's face. She leaned in, her eyes huge. She shot a glance at the front table. She leaned closer, her hair covering her notebook from view. "*Not?*" she whispered.

Malcolm squeaked and quivered. He stretched his paw to the next word.

"A." Amelia breathed.

And the final one. Malcolm shook with excitement. Finally, the world would know. Well, one nutter at least. Gleefully, Malcolm pirouetted on the final word.

"Mouse," Amelia read.

Amelia stared at Malcolm. "Not. A. Mouse. Not a mouse?" she repeated. "What do you mean? You are not a mouse?"

Malcolm made a little bow. It was showing off, but he was so pleased with himself, he could hardly contain it.

From his seat, Jovahn looked over his shoulder at them. Amelia glared at him and pulled her chair in closer.

"Really?" It was Amelia's turn to squeak. "You're not a mouse? Well, what are you then?"

Malcolm had anticipated this question. He tried a flip like Jesses James had done at the Academy meeting the week before. He landed on his stomach, pointing with both paws to the glorious word in the middle of the page.

"Rat."

Amelia started to laugh out loud, then covered her mouth. "A *rat*? You're a rat? You're Malcolm the *Rat*?"

Jovahn scooted his chair back. "What're you doing?"

Amelia frowned. "My reading! Go away!" She turned her back on him.

Malcolm was nearly delirious. Malcolm the Rat. Oh crumb, that had a delicious sound to it!

The class began stirring. From your front table, Mr. Binney, you called out, "All right, everyone. Time to get ready to go. Amelia, is Malcolm out of his cage?"

Amelia scooped Malcolm up and put him back in the cage. "He was helping me read," she said, as she took out her assignment notebook. "Mr. Binney, are we having our social studies test Monday instead of Tuesday? Because I was thinking, since we have that assembly . . ."

You ran your hand through your hair. "Oh, that's right. Okay, class . . ."

As the rest of the class filled out their assignment notebooks and packed up their books, Amelia scribbled on a piece of paper. Then the bell rang. Amelia scraped her chair back and stood with everyone else. And just as Malcolm thought that maybe Amelia would leave without another word, she slipped the paper into Malcolm's cage. "See you Monday, Malcolm," she said, with a pat on the wire grid.

Malcolm sniffed the lump of folded paper. A note! As the ears, eyes, nose, and whiskers of Room 11, he'd seen enough of those being passed around to recognize one. Malcolm grabbed it and buried it deep in the shredded paper of the corner of his cage. He'd have to read it later, once everyone had left.

It could be a while. Part of the day's routine was you staying late, Mr. Binney. Every night, without fail. Past dark sometimes. But Malcolm had noticed that you never left until a woman with curly red hair and a shiny loop through her eyebrow pushed a cart into the room. Her name was Ms. Brumble. And every night, as she entered the room, she'd present a green apple[21] to you, like it was a hard-earned sticker on a behavior mod chart. You'd smile and nudge her into your shabby brown teacher chair. She'd put her feet up on her desk the exact same way Jovahn always tries to. But you never seemed to mind when she did it. Then you'd take the broom off her cart and sweep the room. And when she left, that's when you'd go, too. But never before.

See? Malcolm was a natural for the ears, eyes, and nose of Room 11.[22] You also can see that Malcolm had a while to go before he could crack open Amelia's note. But that was okay. He was happy thinking about Amelia and his rattiness for the time being. He still didn't have anything for the Midnight Academy meeting that night, but maybe something would turn up. Meanwhile, someone in the world knew he was a rat. A rat! And she wasn't repulsed. No, in fact . . . well, this was probably premature, but Malcolm felt like grinning. Like you always do, Mr. Binney, after Ms. Brumble leaves for the night. He felt like maybe he had made his first friend at McKenna.

And with that delicious thought, Malcolm did what any self-respecting rat who had spent all day awake and

---

[21] Granny Smith, right?

[22] Not the whiskers part so much.

alert (well, mostly) and had time to kill would do. While you waited for Ms. Brumble to come by the room—still peeking in that little square fuzzy box, from time to time—Malcolm dragged his Comf-E-Cube over the spot where he had buried Amelia's note. And he snuggled in deep for a long, satisfied nap.

CHAPTER 6
THE GRUMBLE OF THE BRUMBLE

Have you ever gone to sleep feeling like you had had the most perfect day and that yes, indeed, you might be a rat (or person) of valor and merit? And then suddenly you bolt up in bed, hours later, awake and horrified at something terrible that you'd forgotten? Something that probably was the opposite of valor and merit?

Yeah, well that didn't happen to Malcolm.[23]

It probably should have, and it would have changed everything in the story, but it didn't. Malcolm slept hard and sound with the glow of a new friendship. The only thing that woke him later was the ringing of the Midnight Academy bell.

---

[23] Did you catch what Malcolm had done? If not, you'll just have to keep reading.

Malcolm jerked awake so fast that he smacked his head on his water bottle. It dripped in his eyes. Crumb—no time for Amelia's note now! And Malcolm couldn't be late to his first official Midnight Academy meeting. All he could do was pat the shredded paper over the note and sneak out into the darkness of McKenna School at midnight.

"And here's the school office. Jesse James and Billy the Kid are the ones in charge of communications. They ring the bell at midnight for us, too. And, of course, they know all the emergency codes." After a short pause for Malcolm to peek in, Aggy whisked along on the tile floor, her long tail swinging from side to side briskly. Malcolm scampered to keep up. Gristle, his feet were sore. The Academy meeting that night had turned out to be a tour of the school with Aggy, Jesse, and Billy while the rest of the group met in the library. So far, Malcolm had been through every supply closet, classroom, and teacher workroom on the first two floors. He had never walked so much in his life.[24]

Aggy continued, "We've raised our security level from Lemon to Tangerine. But I'm sure Honey Bunny went over all that with you last week."

Malcolm swallowed, thinking about Honey Bunny and their conversation. "Um, sure."

---

[24] Remember how much Kiera complained about the walking on the nature center field trip? Malcolm felt a little like that, only he didn't gripe about it. And he wasn't wearing jeweled flip-flops in the woods.

Suddenly, Aggy stopped. Malcolm ran right into her scaly bottom. "Oops. Sorry, Aggy. I guess I'm a little tired—" The words died in Malcolm's throat.

Aggy tilted her head. Her tongue flicked in and out. Malcolm saw that Jesse and Billy had stopped their game of tag and were watching Aggy with a seriousness he hadn't seen on their faces before. Then there was a flicker, and the long row of lights down the center of the hallway lit up! "I thought things were clear!" She shot a glance at Jesse. "Didn't you call a Limp Lettuce?"

"It was! I did. Someone's come back!" Jesse squeaked. Billy darted to the shadows. Malcolm froze in the light. Even though Malcolm had always been a pet, he *knew*. He knew that being caught out in the open—in the light—well, it's deep and it's instinctual: It's a rat's worst nightmare.

Aggy must have sensed Malcolm's panic. Before he could bolt, she curled her long tail protectively around Malcolm and hissed, "Hush." Her forked tongue tickled the inside of Malcolm's ear. "She's checking on us. She does sometimes. You'll have to run, run quickly! Through there. Follow Jesse and Billy. Go!"

"But—" Through the floor, Malcolm felt footsteps getting closer. He pawed at his whiskers, but they were already chewed down to spiky bristles.

"Go!" And with that, Aggy snapped her tail and released Malcolm. The power in her tail flung Malcolm yards down the hall. He scampered through the door. It was a small cloakroom, bursting with mounds of boots, mittens, lunch bags, and coats.

Billy pulled Malcolm deep into the pile. "Here. Burrow."

Malcolm stuck his head in a fur-lined boot. *Phew!* An odor even worse than that time Jovahn took off his sneakers in class enveloped Malcolm. His eyes watered. He popped his head back up, gasping for air. Aggy was there now. She shoved him back down with a clawed foot. "Burrow!"

Malcolm burrowed.

He heard Aggy wiggle behind a cabinet in the back of the closet.

Pad, pad, pad. Footsteps.

Malcolm's nose twitched. Lemon cleaning solution and pencil shavings. He knew that smell. Ms. Brumble? It hadn't occurred to Malcolm that Ms. Brumble belonged anywhere else but with her feet up on your desk in Room 11, Mr. Binney. A flashlight beam stabbed the darkness of the small room. Malcolm held his breath.

Finally, after what seemed like ages, the hall light went out. The footsteps retreated. A few minutes later, there was the now familiar buzz and click of the school's locks. Still, Malcolm waited until Jesse stuck his head in the boot and called, "You okay, Malcolm?"

Malcolm crawled out. Jesse and Billy and Aggy already stood on the floor next to the pile. "What is this place?" he asked. Crumb, he could still smell boot stench. He licked the back of his paw and made a face. Was it stuck to his fur now?

Aggy's tongue flicked. "It's one of our Niches. A safe spot in the building to hide. To store our equipment. The lankies and nutters call this one the Lost and Found."

Billy piped up. "It's practically our vacation home. Our playground! No one ever comes in here. And it's all fleecy soft." She took a running leap into the pile.

"Cheez. How impulsive," Jesse scolded. Then he grinned and somersaulted in, too.

Aggy cleared her throat and Billy peeked out from a fleece hat. Jesse popped his head out of the pile. "We're coming, we're coming."

Aggy pointed to something scratched into the wall near the bottom of the door frame. "You should know this, Malcolm. These are Marks. To lankies or nutters, they mean nothing. But to critters, well, they can literally save your life."

Malcolm peered at the one on the Lost and Found door jamb. It looked like this:

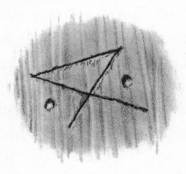

Aggy continued, "This is our Mark for safety. If you ever see a grid." She drew her claws across the floor.

"It means the Niche has been found and is unsafe. Be very careful."

Jesse and Billy had finally come out of the pile of clothes. They watched Aggy's foot. "And if you see this." She drew a circle with two arrows.

"Get out—fast," Jesse said.

"Most critters who make that mark—well, it's the last thing they do alive. A sacrifice for the rest of the critters of the Academy," Billy added quietly. There was a moment of silence.

Malcolm cleared his throat. "The lanky who peeked in here, she was . . . Ms. Brumble?"

Aggy nodded and Jesse groaned. "The Grumble of the Brumble!"

Aggy said, "*Ms.* Brumble is the night custodian. She takes care of the building, until about eleven o'clock. Be very careful around her. Very careful. She's not exactly an enemy—because she has the school's best interest at heart, too—but, in many ways, we're at odds with her. It's why we're at Tangerine Alert Levels right now. Jesse here stole her cell phone a few weeks ago—"

"For Academy communications!" Jesse cried. "And she lost it first."

His sister gave him a playful punch. "She dropped it in the hall. And you stole it before she could even turn around to pick it up. Now she's been extra nosy ever since."

"We need it!" Jesse sulked, swatting Billy back. "We need it to move the Academy into the twenty-first century." He sounded an awful lot like Grumble of the Brumble himself.

Aggy sighed. "It *is* useful. Still, she's been looking for it after hours—that's probably why she was poking around here."

Aggy considered and seemed about to say something, but before she could, Jesse leaped in front of her. "Not to change the subject, but, Malcolm—is that swillerific smell coming from you?"

Billy held her nose. "I didn't want to say anything before—you know, I have much better manners than my brother, but—woo-*whee!* You stink, Malcolm!"

Malcolm felt himself go pink around the whiskers. "It was the boot. The boot I burrowed in!"

Billy hooted. Jesse snorted with laughter. Malcolm looked to Aggy. She shook her head and rolled her eyes. "Don't look at me, Malcolm. I live with kindergartners every day. They're nothing compared to these two." Aggy cleared her throat. "Okay now. I think Malcolm's had enough for one night. Jesse, Billy, why don't you sound the All Clear for anyone else who was out in the building. I'll walk Malcolm back up to his room. Then I need to get under my heat lamp."

"Yes, sir—I mean, ma'am—I mean, reptile," said Jesse, cracking Billy up all over again. He and his sister scampered off toward the office, leaving the hall strangely quiet and almost lonely.

"What's a heat lamp?" Malcolm asked, trotting alongside Aggy. Malcolm had noticed that as the night went on, Aggy was moving slower and slower. He thought it was for his sake, but now he could see that she was stiff, too.

Aggy smiled. "I'm cold-blooded. So the colder the air is, the colder and slower I am. It's okay," she added at the concerned look in Malcolm's eyes. "I have my heat lamp, and you—well, you're warm-blooded and make your own heat. Besides, you're a rodent. Mice are hardy. Rats, too, for that matter. But I'm cold-blooded. Cold-blooded and old. Now, here you go." They had arrived at Room 11.

Aggy's comment reminded Malcolm about something else. Could he ask her? "Aggy, I can't help wondering. Why does everyone hate rats?"

Aggy sighed. "Oh, Malcolm. Rats are complicated. There was a rat in the Academy once. A long time ago. It didn't work out, but don't worry about it. It's nothing to do with you. You've got an amazing Knack—and a natural instinct. You showed that tonight."

Malcolm hesitated. "But—it's not only the Academy."

Aggy lowered her head so her face was even with Malcolm's. He stared into her orange eyes. "Malcolm. You'll do fine. Do what you think is right. That's all anyone can ask for." She scooted him a little with her tail. "Now, get back to your cage." Malcolm started into the room, then Aggy called after him, "Oh, and Malcolm?"

Malcolm turned. Aggy's mouth curled upward. "You may want to—what do you mammals call it? *Groom* a little before the next meeting. You *do* have a certain odor about you." Then she whisked her tail around and lumbered off down to the kindergarten rooms.

As he licked himself down in his cage, Malcolm thought about what Aggy had said. In a lot of ways, it sounded like what you had said, Mr. Binney, about being the fifth-grader you wanted to be. But both you and Aggy made it sound so simple. And so far, life at McKenna had been anything but simple.

And it was about to get more complicated. After what Malcolm assumed was the real Limp Lettuce bell, and after Malcolm finally felt like he wasn't polluting the air around him with his boot stench, he dug up Amelia's note. And as he did, he finally remembered something. Something that should have woken him up from his long nap before. Something you've probably already figured out, Mr. Binney.

The Academy handbook. And the Academy bylaws. Malcolm was pretty sure that right before Honey Bunny had tackled him and made him swear he was a mouse and not a rat, Malcolm had been reading—reading something very important.

Something like, *"Never communicate with humans."*

Oh, gristle. Being the rat he wanted to be was not going to be easy.

CHAPTER 7
THE NOSH AND FODDER TOUR

Now, I know, Mr. Binney, that you're probably thinking that Malcolm should have admitted to the Academy what he had done, aren't you? After all, being truthful was part of being the fifth-grader—rat—Malcolm wanted to be. And it was the right thing to do.

But.

Well, Malcolm *did* consider it. And granted, in light of what happened later, it would have all worked out much better if he had. But here's what else he was thinking: Malcolm was thinking maybe the Academy would never know—I mean, really, how could they find out? Amelia was the only one who knew. And it wasn't like Amelia was going to tromp into another classroom, start chatting to that pet, and then blab about Malcolm.

And Malcolm confessing his mistake—at the third Academy meeting he'd ever attended, no less—well, wouldn't that solidify Honey Bunny's suspicion that Malcolm was a rat? Well, Malcolm *was* a rat, but not *that* kind of a rat—a no-good, not-to-be-trusted dirty rat *fink*.

Malcolm nibbled his stubbly whiskers, thinking about all this.

Finally, he decided there was nothing he could do right away, anyway. He might as well open Amelia's note.

Malcolm unfolded it, but it was too dark in the room. Rats don't need a lot of light to get around. They mostly depend on their sense of feel and smell and hearing. But you do need light to read, even if you have a Knack.

Malcolm folded the note back up. For lack of a better place, he tucked it in his cheek. Then, for the second time that night, he crawled out of his cage. He could see the hall night-lights were on. Maybe he could read it out there.

Malcolm slid under the space beneath the door.

And as soon as he stepped out into the hall, he was bowled over by Jesse James and Billy the Kid.

"Hey!" Billy the Kid said, skidding to a stop. "Malcolm! We were just coming for you. Now that Aggy's asleep, we're here to give you the unofficial tour. The Nosh and Fodder tour!"

Malcolm coughed. He had almost swallowed the note!

He opened his mouth to say something, but before he could, Jesse butted in. "Uh-huh! Only we rodents understand the true art of nibbling, right? Right? Are we right? So we thought we'd come by to ask: Malcolm, have you ever heard of a corn dog?"

Billy pretended to swoon. "Oh, sweet driblets. *Corn dogs.*"

Malcolm's stomach lurched and rumbled. It had been such a long time since he'd eaten. Was it only earlier that day he had turned down Amelia's graham cracker? What had he been thinking?

"Come on, Malcolm." Billy took off running. "Wait'll you try tater tots! Come on!"

Malcolm felt the note in his cheek. He considered spitting it out and hiding it in the hall. But what if someone found it? He didn't even know what it said. And Jesse and Billy were right. Nibbling *was* a passion of Malcolm's. So he stashed the note in his other cheek and scampered after them.

They went down the stairs and through a long hallway. The three rodents turned the corner and stopped abruptly at the entrance of a huge room. Rows of long tables spidered out on one side. On the other, gleaming silver counters and cabinets. A smell of deep grease, canned peaches, and ketchup nearly knocked Malcolm over.

"Behold," Jesse said, spreading his paws wide on the slightly sticky floor. "The Nosh and Fodder."

"The cafeteria," Billy said breathlessly.

"Spread out and explore," Jesse called. He launched into a flattened french fry. "Just don't eat so much we have to carry you home."

Oh crumblity-crumbs! Literally, the *crumbs!* Back by the garbage cans, morsels, shreds, specks, leftovers, scraps, driblets, and nubbins of every variety. Peas. Bits of taco shells. Muffin fragments. Grilled cheese crusts. And the smells. Malcolm didn't have names for them all but they swirled and danced in his nose—and he wanted to eat them all. He slurped up a little drool and realized his mouth was hanging wide open.

At this rate, Amelia's note would be too soggy to read. Malcolm had to find a place to hide it. Then he'd enjoy a little Nosh. And a little Fodder. He skirted around the first counter and headed toward the back corner. There, in the shadows of the kitchen, he banged up against a metal sliding door in the wall.

Ouch. Malcolm promised himself again he'd stop chewing his whiskers. Who knew whiskers were so important outside of a cage?

The sliding door was open a crack. Malcolm scooted through it and found a wire folding gate behind the door and a tiny room behind that. Boxes of cleaning supplies were stacked on the right side. Perfect. He nestled the note behind a plastic crate. Shredded taco cheese crumbs, watch out!

"Hey, Malcolm, where are you? Don't go . . ." Malcolm heard Billy's muffled voice, but he couldn't make out what she was saying.

"In here," he called. "I think it's some kind of storage room. The ra—guys—at the Pet Emporium were always talking about storage rooms—"

Just then Malcolm felt a hum through his paws. A motor under the little room kicked into gear. The floor clanged and creaked and, with a jolt, started rising!

"Hey! Help!" Malcolm cried. He ran to the door, but only in time to glimpse Jesse and Billy disappearing beneath him. He was going up!

"Malcolm!" one of them called. Then they slipped out of sight.

Up, up he went. After a minute or so, he passed by another sliding door. Then another. Would it ever stop?

But just as Malcolm thought he'd never get back to Room 11, the floor shuddered to a halt. In the darkness, Malcolm could see another folding metal gate, and then an identical heavy sliding door—that led to where? A dim light shone through a crack in it.

Gristle. Now what had he gotten himself into?

Malcolm instinctively froze, waiting to hear and feel and smell what was next. But it was quiet and all he could smell was the box of plastic sporks next to him. He'd have to venture out. What if someone missed him? An escaped pet—even a mouse—would be disastrous.

Malcolm took a deep breath and squeezed out. He immediately sneezed. A thick layer of dust coated everything. Malcolm looked behind him and saw a trail of his own footprints.

Where was he? Not anywhere that Aggy had taken him on his tour. He was a floor or two above all that. Ancient shelves lined these walls. Boxes and books crammed the floor. And it was eerily silent.

Suddenly, a shriek pierced the quiet. Malcolm jumped. What was that? Not any lanky or nutter. It didn't sound nearby, but Malcolm's passion for nibbling evaporated. He had to get out of there and back down to Room 11. Fast.

Malcolm scurried along the edge of the room. On the far side was a door. He took a deep breath and squeezed under it.

As he came out the other side, at first Malcolm thought

he was in some sort of jungle. Stacks of broken chalk-boards, overturned chairs, science lab tables lying on their sides, and empty file cabinets were all jammed together, covering the floor. Supplies, too. Boxes of chalk. Crates of hand sanitizer. The only light was an emergency exit sign hanging from the ceiling. It cast a dull red glow over the broken landscape.

It was cluttered, but Malcolm actually breathed a sigh of relief. Clutter meant lots of hiding places. Also, he saw that if you took out all the mess, this was a floor like the ones below that he had toured. He must be on one of the no-longer-used upper floors. So the stairs must be in the same location they were on the first floor, right? Malcolm headed down the hall.

As he stepped out, his paws stirred up the clouds of dust. Wafts of stale air and dampness swirled around him. Malcolm found himself running from the safety of one shadow to the next.

Scurry, scurry, leap. Pause. Pant, pant, pant. Listen. Once he thought he heard a basketball dribbling. But he realized it was his heart hammering in his chest.

And then—then he heard voices.

Malcolm froze. But there was no mistake. An urgent voice asked, "Did you see him? Why didn't you try to stop him?"

Malcolm held his breath and crept forward. Under a teacher desk with a broken leg. "Up the elevator?" he heard.

As Malcolm crept closer, the voices sounded louder, but hollower, too—like they came from far away. As he squeezed under the edge of the desk at the end of the hallway, Malcolm came face to face with a boxlike contraption under the window. He could feel the heat coming from it and hear the hiss of water being boiled into steam. A radiator. Malcolm had learned about radiators earlier that week.[25]

The voices were wafting through the floor under the radiator.

"We need to get him out of there!" Was that Aggy?

"Oh, it's my fault," he heard her continue. "I should have warned him. Do you think he made it?"

Malcolm realized with a start that she was talking about him. He swelled a little at the concern he heard in her voice.

"Suspicious, if you ask me," said a deeper, gruffer voice. Honey Bunny. "What's he doing up there anyway? Already he can read, and we catch him going upstairs on purpose. It makes me wonder. Maybe it's not the first time he's been up there. Maybe he *came* from up there. We know Snip is working on something. Then *he* shows up. Maybe they're in cahoots."

There was that name again. Who *was* Snip?

"Oh, nonsense," Aggy said. "Have you seen the cage

---

[25] Remember Skylar's crayon "waterfall" and the lecture about not keeping things on the radiator, Mr. Binney? That took him ages to clean up.

they have for him in Room Eleven? He's doted on. He's a pet. No, it's my fault."

Malcolm stumbled up to the radiator, pressed his face near the pipe, and called down, "Hey, I can hear you. I'm up here. I'm okay. I'm—I'm finding my way back down."

"Malcolm, are you all right?" He heard Jesse's voice float up.

Then a growl from Honey Bunny: "Malcolm, get down here. You don't know what you're doing—"

Just then, the hairs of the back of Malcolm's neck stood on end. Malcolm didn't know how he knew, but something was different. And it was then that he saw it. Carved into the paint of the radiator. The Mark.

Get out—fast.

At that exact time, a throat cleared behind Malcolm. Then it spoke—hoarse, barely above a whisper. "I think you might stay."

Malcolm's mouth went dry. He turned, but whoever or whatever was behind him was well hidden. Then he heard all four voices from the pipe—Billy, Jesse, Aggy, even Honey Bunny—scream: "Malcolm, run!"

CHAPTER 8
SNIP

Malcolm didn't wait for a second opinion or even a second breath. He aimed himself at the red glow of the exit sign over the stairs and he sprinted. He leaped over a rolled-up map and spun out on a piece of chalk. Behind him, whatever it was, was bigger. Malcolm could hear that it took different routes than he did. But it stayed close.

Finally! The stairs. Malcolm tore down the first set, skidding wide on the turn of the landing. As he did, he threw a glance over his shoulder.

A cat. A *cat!* A black cat, streaking toward him. Just a darker spot in the shadows. Malcolm spun around the landing and, skipping every other step, jumped onto the floor below.

But this wasn't his floor either! It was another storage

area, although less dusty and forlorn as the one above it. Malcolm's claws slid on the tile as he tried to turn the corner to go down another set of stairs. But he was going too fast. He slammed into a plastic storage tub.

The cat pounced. But the plastic tub gave Malcolm something to push off from. Malcolm launched himself down the second flight. He didn't need to look behind him to check this time—he could feel the cat breathing on the back of his neck.

He wasn't fast enough! Malcolm tumbled and bounced down to the next landing—finally, there was his floor! And the Academy, waiting.

"Malcolm, hurry!" he heard Billy call.

Malcolm rolled over and flung himself down this last flight of stairs. But he didn't go anywhere. Instead, pain seared through his finally healed tail. A glance behind him nearly made him faint. The cat had Malcolm's tail neatly pinned against the cold tile step with her overlong claws.

Malcolm wiggled and writhed, trying to get free. The cat laughed. A horrible sound—wheezy and tight and tormented. "Are you sure you want to leave?" It was that same horrible, hoarse voice. And then Malcolm saw it. A collar so tight, it cut into the cat's skin at her neck. Malcolm shuddered and squeezed his eyes shut.

He curled into a ball. Surely, sharp teeth would pierce him next.

But . . . they didn't. Malcolm cracked his eyes open.

The cat wasn't even looking at Malcolm. She was staring at the bottom of the steps.

At Aggy.

Aggy's spiky ruff was raised. She hissed, a noise that made Malcolm flinch. "Get out of here," she snarled at the cat. "You don't belong on this floor."

The cat arched her back and hissed back. Malcolm could smell her stale breath. It reminded him of spiders and dust.

There was a moment that seemed as long to Malcolm as the minute before recess does to a nutter.

Then the cat lifted her paw. She hissed again—and batted Malcolm down the remaining stairs, where he thumped to a halt in a tangle of tail and legs. He looked up.

The landing was empty. The cat was gone.

Malcolm gasped and gingerly stood on wobbly legs. "The cat . . ." he panted. It sounded too incredible to be true. Had it really happened that way? "The cat wouldn't come down to this floor."

Aggy's ruff folded back. She nodded. "Blessed greens. You made it. Maybe you have two Knacks." She curled her tail around Malcolm.

Honey Bunny, who had been staring up the stairs, tapped his massive hind paw on the floor. "Huh. Escaped. From Snip." He jabbed in Malcolm's direction. "Or maybe this was all part of some plan."

Malcolm bristled. "What? I was almost eaten! What—that was Snip?"

Honey Bunny ignored the question. Instead, he muttered, "Makes everything more believable if you come back hurt a little."

But Aggy was studying Malcolm. "Come, we'll escort you back to your room. You're very lucky, you know."

She nodded at Billy and Jesse. They gave a little wave. "See you, Malcolm."

For the second time that night, Aggy walked Malcolm back to Room 11. This time, Honey Bunny lumbered along

74

behind him. Malcolm felt a little like a nutter being escorted to the principal's office.

But as they arrived outside Room 11, Aggy turned and said, "To answer your question simply: Yes, that cat is Snip. But there's more to that answer than I can give you in a few minutes' time. Look, you're shivering. You need to get back to your cage. You've had quite the night—a lanky and then Snip! Let's see, tomorrow's Friday. Do the nutters take you home for the weekend?"

Malcolm shook his head.

"Good. Now, Honey Bunny and I have a district meeting tomorrow night, but let's you and I meet Saturday. Come to my classroom, 1B, first floor. Around eleven? We'll talk."

Honey Bunny stopped hopping. Malcolm could see his claws extend on his front paws. "Are you kidding, Aggy? You're going to fill the *mouse* in on Academy secrets? After what happened with the last pledge?"

Aggy leveled one of her orange eyes at the rabbit. "That doesn't mean it'll happen again, Honey Bunny. He's been to the Fourth. And returned. Maybe he can help. She's up to something—you said it yourself. Collecting things, moving them around the building. We know that. But what is she doing? Maybe he saw something."

Malcolm wanted to say that he didn't care. That his life was perfectly happy in Room 11 and he wasn't planning on leaving it again. In fact, right now, the most adventure

Malcolm ever wanted again was a wild-berry frosted Pop-Tart.

But something about Honey Bunny stirred Malcolm up. Every time Honey Bunny spoke to him or about him, Malcolm felt the same as when Skylar reached in and petted his fur in the wrong direction. Malcolm truly had no desire to find out more about that cat—he longed to be safe in his Comf-E-Cube, except . . . if Honey Bunny was so against him knowing . . . well, then maybe Malcolm *did* want to. I guess that's one way Malcolm was very like fifth grade nutters.

"Now, here we are," Aggy said as they drew up to Room 11's door. "I trust that you can find your own way back to your cage." The orange eyes bored into him. "This time, no detours. No Nosh and Fodder. Not even at the classroom snack cabinet." Malcolm felt vaguely insulted and guilty at the same time. But mostly tired. Very, very tired. "I'll see you tomorrow night," Aggy said.

Malcolm nodded. As he slid under the door, he could hear Honey Bunny's grumble as the two Academy elders retreated down the hall.

Malcolm limped into Room 11. He heaved himself into his cage and licked his shredded tail. He fell asleep so fast, he didn't realize that he had left the door of his cage cracked open.

And he slept so hard, he barely stirred when someone stopped in front of it.

Do you know who it was, Mr. Binney? It wasn't you,

of course. You were long gone home. And it wasn't a cat named Snip from the Fourth. It wasn't even an Academy member.

No, late that night someone else was in Room 11.

That someone frowned at Malcolm's open door when she saw it. "The last thing he needs is you getting out." But instead of closing it, she reached in and placed a finger lightly on Malcolm's back. Malcolm finally came fully awake with a whiff of pencil shavings and lemon cleaning solution.

That's right. Did you know she visited your room sometimes after you left, Mr. Binney?

"You critters are more trouble than you're worth, you know," the Grumble of the Brumble grumbled. But she rubbed him behind his ears. He tried not to wiggle, to shiver, but *crumb*, he felt as warm and as melty as a stick of gum in a back pocket.

Then, after another stroke or two, Ms. Brumble snapped the latch on the cage door and strode out of the room. The door clicked shut behind her.

And Malcolm was left wondering if he had dreamed the whole thing.

CHAPTER 9
LEAP! CREEP! KEEP!

Malcolm settled into a dull Saturday. He slept in, dozing in the sun. He accidentally ate his whole weekend's worth of kibble by noon. Then he plopped in his shredded paper for another long nap. Except for the lack of video games, his Saturday probably wasn't all that much different from most fifth-graders'.

Finally, when the room grew dark, Malcolm stirred. He pushed open the latch on his door and wandered out. To be honest, he was still kind of hoping to find something noteworthy to bring to the Midnight Academy to impress everyone. But he was also scared. After all, he'd almost been eaten by a cat the last time he ventured out. So Malcolm looked around, but he kept within a dash and a leap of his cage.

Malcolm poked under the back counter. A stick of gum lay forgotten near the wall.

He pawed at the wrapper. Watermelon mango blast. Hmm. He took a tiny nibble.

Oh, sweet nubbins.

The flavor exploded in his head. No wonder the nutters were so cheezy for gum! Malcolm sank his incisors[26] into a bigger chunk. He chewed. And chewed.

The flavor. Magical. And the chew! It never went away!

There was still an hour left[27] before it was time to meet Aggy in the kindergarten room. Malcolm returned to his table. He chomped his gum and flipped through a little more of Amelia's copy of *Despereaux*. Crumb, the mice weren't very nice critters in that story either. And the lankies were worse.

Finally, the clock pointed to eleven. By now, the gum felt and tasted like a lump of pencil eraser. He spit it out and tried to stick it to the bottom of a desk, like he had seen Kiera do, but it got tangled in his stubbly whiskers. Malcolm swiped at them. Now it was on his fur! Gristle,

---

[26] Again, I have to say that if anyone ever took a close look at Malcolm's teeth, they'd have no doubt he was a rat. No mouse has the power he does behind those chompers. Believe me, I know.

[27] Part of the last Academy meeting had been an explanation of telling time. Maybe you should have Aggy teach "quarter to" and "quarter after" sometime to Skylar, Mr. Binney.

how did the nutters manage this stuff? Strings of sticky pink stretched from paw to paw.

Malcolm rubbed the gum off as best he could on Skylar's sweatshirt,[28] then he scampered out the door. He couldn't be late. Not for Aggy.

In the hall, everything looked bigger and darker than the night before. Every little scratch and tap of Malcolm's claws echoed in the empty space. Malcolm couldn't help but wonder who might be listening to him scuttle down the hall. Academy critters? Or maybe a cat with a too-tight collar? He hurried faster and sucked on a gummy whisker.

Malcolm trotted down the stairs to the kindergarten hall. Was it his nerves or was this floor of the school a lot colder than the fifth grade one? It felt like the postrecess blast of air the nutters always brought in.

Room 1B. Malcolm stopped. On either side of the door, construction paper jack-o'-lanterns leered at him. Malcolm could see that the kindergartners still had a ways to go on their cutting skills.

Cool air streamed out from the sliver of space beneath the door, bringing with it the scent of lemon cleanser. This door hung much lower than Room 11's though. There was no sneaking under here. How was he supposed to get in?

Malcolm nudged the door with his nose. It had worked for Aggy on his tour the night before. She had explained

---

[28] Truthfully, no one—especially Skylar—would ever notice.

how one of Pete and Octavius's jobs was taping the locks of some of the doors.

Oof. Not this one, apparently. All Malcolm ended up with was a smashed nose.

He shot a look in both directions down the hall. He called out, "Aggy, I'm here." His voice sounded thin and very un-valorous.

Inside the room, he could hear fluttering. "Peep! Peep! Peep!" The chicks.

Malcolm bent his head down. "Aggy," he called through the space under the door. "Aggy, the door is locked."

"Eep! Creep! Heap!" the chicks chirped.

Malcolm sat back on his haunches. Maybe this was some kind of test. Maybe he needed to prove his worthiness to the Academy. To prove he could figure a way in. He could almost picture Honey Bunny's smug look on the other side of the door.

So how else could he get in? Above the door—like all the classrooms—was a rectangular window that tilted out an inch or two. A transom. Malcolm remembered you called it that, Mr. Binney, when you lectured Jovahn about throwing paper airplanes through it.

Malcolm swallowed. It was awfully high. He had to take a step back to see the top.

But he had to try.[29] Malcolm clamored up a coat hanging in a cubby, then leaped across to the wooden door trim. His claws scratched for a moment, then took hold. Seconds later, he was peering through the crack in the transom.

Malcolm glanced back at the hallway and swayed.

Okay, so . . . no looking down.

Malcolm wedged his nose into the window's crack and peered in on the classroom.

"Peep! Steep! Leap!" the chicks cheeped.

"Aggy?" he called. No answer.

He could see her cage near the window, but it was empty. Malcolm shivered. He scampered down the doorway on the other side. The chicks went crazy.

"Eep! Steep! Creep!" The chicks tossed themselves at the side of their wire cage.

---

[29] Malcolm's a lot like Amelia in this way. She doesn't like to not take a challenge either. That's how she and Jovahn got into that very immature staring contest one afternoon. She shouldn't have let Jovahn annoy her into it. She knew better.

"You said that before," Malcolm mumbled. He scouted around a bit. "Where's Aggy?"

"Leap. Creep. Keep!"

"Aggy?" Malcolm called again. A strong scent of lemon cleanser—the same kind Ms. Brumble used to clean desks—hung in the air. But Aggy didn't seem to be in the room. Well, maybe she and Honey Bunny were still on their way. Now what?

As he made his way to the back of the room, he saw the cabinets under the sink were wide open. The contents of a jar of paste dribbled across the floor. Bits of paper and foil were stuck in it—it looked like the scrap box had been tipped over. Lettuce leaves, animal crackers, even some Jolly Ranchers were scattered about. Kindergartners sure were messy.

Malcolm's stomach pinched. He had eaten all that kibble. But that was so long ago! He was practically starving by now. And he was just waiting. Malcolm stole a glance at the door. Still closed. He took a bite of lettuce. It was okay—crispy, but a little watery. He launched himself into the animal crackers.

Ah, crackers. They weren't cinnamon sugar, but still, just the right amount of satisfying crunch. But after a few, Malcolm slowed. He wasn't sure, but something wasn't right. His paws were stiff. His ear tips ached a bit. His nose—it was as cold as an ice pack in a lunch bag.

That was it. That was what was wrong.

Malcolm was cold.

Malcolm had never been cold before. Not really. Not like this, so cold that his paws couldn't quite grasp his cracker the way he needed them to. So cold that his fur had plumped out all over, making him look twice as wide as he was.[30] Malcolm didn't even know his fur could do that.

Anyway, being that cold isn't good. Not when you are inside a classroom.

Something was wrong.

Malcolm set down his cracker and took a few steps to-

---

[30] No, he wasn't extra plump because of all the animal crackers.

ward Aggy's cage. It was on a low table next to the long row of windows. Malcolm pulled himself up the side of a nearby bookcase.

From here, the air was even chillier. And it was no wonder. The bottom half of the window next to Aggy's cage was shattered. The freezing night air blasted in through it.

"Steep! Creep! Keep!" the chicks called again.

Malcolm jumped down to the table, his claws skittering a little on the wood. He tripped on something hard. A chalky white stone rattled to the floor.

A cold knot—colder even than the night air—grew in Malcolm's stomach. It tangled and snarled worse than a kindergartner's shoelace. What was going on here? Where *was* Aggy?

The quietness of the building seemed to press in on Malcolm. He needed to find someone. To tell someone. Something wasn't right here in Room 1B.

Malcolm leaped to the floor. It was a big jump, and his hind legs pushed against a stack of books. The top book, half open and tilted on the top of the pile (in a way Amelia would never tolerate), slowly slid off. Malcolm winced as it fell, cracking into the remaining shards of glass in the window. Outside, Malcolm heard the tinkle of glass hitting the pavement. Oops.

But on the other side of the room, Malcolm heard something else.

The classroom door.

Opening.

CHAPTER 10
THE RAT (FINK)

Honey Bunny stood in the doorway, his rabbit face masked in shadows.

Malcolm ran to him. "Honey Bunny, oh, thank my whiskers! I'm so glad you're here."

He stopped. The outline of the rabbit glowed from the hall light behind him. So still. Malcolm resisted the urge to poke him, to make sure he was real. Instead, he tried again. "Honey Bunny? Something's not right. Have you seen—"

Now Honey Bunny moved. His paw shot out and swatted Malcolm across the face.

Ow! "Wha—"

Honey Bunny growled, "Don't call me that." Then he spit something out.

A soggy wad of paper.

Malcolm's ears drooped as he recognized it. "Oh, scrap," he whispered. How in nubbins had Honey Bunny gotten ahold of Amelia's note?

"Honey Bunny—HB, I . . ." Malcolm's voice faded. In his head, he could see the Academy handbook: *"Never communicate with humans."*

"So it *is* yours," Honey Bunny said. "Jesse and Billy said it couldn't be."

Malcolm pawed at his whiskers. A pink strand of gum stretched out and Malcolm tried to wipe it off on his fur. "I never meant—"

Honey Bunny glared. "You talked to her. It says—"

Malcolm couldn't help it. He peered around at the note. "What does it say? I—I never got to read it."

Honey Bunny's voice was cold. Colder than the air pouring through the room's broken window. "It says that you're a *rat*."

The words splatted into the room like the time Jovahn threw that water balloon in science at Kiera.

A rat.

"Gristle." Malcolm had to sit down on his haunches. His puffed-up-from-the-cold fur deflated.

The rabbit snatched the note up again. "All along—a skuzzy rat. A *lying* skuzzy rat. Just like—well, what else are you lying about?" Honey Bunny tapped his long, powerful hind foot on the ground. Now that Honey Bunny was in the light, he could see. The leg was bandaged up—with pink gauze, no less. In the back of his mind, Malcolm wondered how Honey Bunny had hurt it.

But there were more urgent things to face now. In a small voice, Malcolm said, "Nothing. I'm just a rat. I'm a pet rat who is so tiny that everyone thinks I'm a mouse. But, the note, it's not that bad. We can trust Amelia. She's my friend."

"Your *friend?*" Honey Bunny's tone made Malcolm shrink against the wall. "You're a *pet*. Does a friend lock another friend in a cage?"

"Well, she has to . . ." Honey Bunny's glare made the words fizzle out in Malcolm's mouth.

But hold on a whisker. It was one thing for Honey Bunny to think skuzzy thoughts about Malcolm, but quite another if he was thinking them of Amelia. Amelia of the straight rows of pencils and neat stacks of books! Of the color-coded notebooks, socks, and hair elastics. Of the strawberry shampoo. *Amelia.* Who talked to Malcolm like he was a critter of valor and merit. Malcolm stiffened his ratty spine. He closed his eyes and blurted, "You don't know. Just because the nutters don't like you. Jesse told me—"

Honey Bunny hopped to a whisker's-breadth of Malcolm's face, and Malcolm's eyes snapped open wide. "I don't know? I don't know the sweet whispered secrets of my second-graders? I do know. I know lots of them are in trouble and hurting and sad. I also know some are mean and some are misunderstood and some are too busy to

89

know I even exist. But I also know that I'm still a pet. Pets have their purpose, and it can be a noble one, but do not confuse it with friendship."

Malcolm's mouth was dry. Maybe there wasn't a way to explain it, but he did know that he and Amelia were different. He knew it down to the tip of his very sore tail.

Honey Bunny stepped back and eyed Malcolm like a nutter who had unpacked stewed spinach for a snack. "You know, Aggy was ready to take you under her scales. And now this. Do you know what can happen if you talk to nutters? It's not critter-wise! If the lankies knew we could talk—" He huffed air out of his pink mouth. "It upsets the balance. We're no longer secret. The Academy's whole work is in jeopardy now." He shook his head. "A rat fink, all along."

Malcolm's whiskers and tail wilted. But—wait. Malcolm raised his head. "Aggy doesn't know?"

"Know? Why do you think I came? I'm not here to sing Christmas carols." And Honey Bunny pushed past Malcolm into the classroom.

Malcolm hurried after him. "But Aggy's not here. I was coming to tell someone—*oof!*"

Honey Bunny had come to an abrupt halt. Malcolm mashed into his fuzzy rear end.

Malcolm looked around the huge rabbit to the mess of paste and paper and crackers and Jolly Ranchers on the floor. The coldness in the air felt like a weight, pressing him down. He smelled the chemical lemon of cleanser. Heard the frantic calls of the chicks. It seemed obvious now. Of *course* something was terribly wrong here. How could Malcolm have missed it before? And where *was* Aggy?

Honey Bunny slowly pivoted around to Malcolm. "What exactly were you coming to say, rat?"

"That—that Aggy is gone. That the window is broken."

"The window?" Honey Bunny loped to Aggy's cage. "By claw," Honey Bunny swore under his breath.

The rabbit glanced around, then hopped over to the desk. He jumped to the chair, then the desktop. He grabbed a dry-erase marker with his teeth. He knocked the phone off the hook and punched in a series of numbers with the marker. He pressed his fuzzy lips to the phone. "Ripe Tomato. 1B." The words squawked out of the PA system in the wall.

Only then did Honey Bunny hop back down and over to where Malcolm sat, frozen. Malcolm had been hoping that Honey Bunny was going to take charge and make things right here. But that snarled-up kindergarten shoelace feeling in Malcolm's stomach was growing worse, especially the way Honey Bunny was looking at him. Malcolm squirmed.

Finally, Honey Bunny drawled, "What exactly have you done in here, rat?"

The chicks chose that moment to pipe up. "Leap. Creep. Keep!"

Now Malcolm could hear the *pitter-pat, pitter-pat*. The scrape and thud of paws and claws on tile floor. Ripe Tomato. Of course, a code. A summons.

One by one, the rest of the critters hopped, scampered, and crawled into the room.

"What's up, HB?" Jesse asked, a little breathless, spitting out a string that was tied to a scooter from the gym. Pete and Tank sat aboard. Ripe Tomato must mean get here—fast. Not at hermit crab and turtle speeds.

Honey Bunny eyed each one of them. "Any of you critters seen Aggy tonight?" The Academy members shook their heads.

Harriet stepped forward. "What's this about, HB?" she wheezed. "I had an hour left to snooze before our subcommittee meeting—"

Honey Bunny cut her off. "Aggy's gone. Missing."

The Academy stirred. "Missing? What do you mean?" Billy asked.

"I mean, she's not here. She didn't report to the Ripe Tomato. Something's happened to her." He stepped back and gestured his paw at Malcolm. "That's not all. I found this, this *rat*—Malcolm—here. Alone. Inside a locked room. A locked room that's been vandalized, including a window broken from the inside."

What? Malcolm felt like the time he had been zapped by static electricity after Skylar rubbed his shoes on the rug.

The rest of the Academy was just as shocked. "What? A rat?" They all drew back from him. Not a lot. An observer probably wouldn't have noticed, but Malcolm felt it.

Honey Bunny nodded and nudged the folded note on the floor. "Yes, he's a rat. He's been lying to us. And worse—talking to nutters—and who knows who else? Maybe Snip." He gestured to the lettuce leaves. "It's him. He did this. There's gum all over the spilled stuff on the floor. The cage and window, too."

"What?" Malcolm felt the Academy's eyes take in his sticky whiskers. He fought the urge to wipe his face. Gristle, that stupid gum! "But—I was meeting Aggy. It was like this already. Really!" He turned to the chicks. "Tell them!"

The chicks flapped around. "Peep! Steep! Leap!"

Honey Bunny nodded. "Exactly. As I was saying . . ."

"Aw, come on, HB," Jesse said. "Maybe—"

Honey Bunny shook his head. "He's a rat, Jess. He said so himself. He lied. You don't know rats like I do. It's all about survival for them. They'll do whatever it takes to get their next meal, their next breath. They're cunning, sly creatures. Not to be trusted. We've seen it before. I don't know what it is he got out of this, but Aggy's the one who's paid for it. That's why I've called you here."

"But—" Malcolm tried again.

Honey Bunny jabbed at Malcolm with his front paw. "We'll deal with you later. We've got more pressing business." He turned to the others. "We've got to find Aggy. You know she can't last long at night without her heat lamp."

The words sent a jolt through Malcolm and seemed to mobilize the group, too. They formed into teams. Jesse and Billy shot down the hall. Polly and Tank took off at a slower speed after them, with Tank trudging along and Polly flitting in circles above him. Harriet sniffed and lumbered out the door in the other direction. Octavius crawled straight up the wall and disappeared into the ceiling tiles. Malcolm looked around to see how he could help, too, when—*yeow!*

"Not so fast, rat." The voice was low, barely above a whisper, and slightly accented.[31]

Malcolm turned. Pete, the hermit crab, had the end of Malcolm's tail pinched in his claw. The big one.

"I think you'll be heading back to your cage. Until we want to talk to you again." He tugged on Malcolm's tail and Malcolm squeaked in pain. "Let's go."

Malcolm hobbled out the door and back into the dark hall.

Oh, scrap.

---

[31] Caribbean, maybe? Pete came from a beach in Jamaica, it turns out.

CHAPTER 11
A SMALL BLUE BOX

Malcolm waited in his cage, licking off all that gristly gum. He waited and waited. The sun came up Sunday morning. Then it grew dark and dim Sunday night. The whole time Malcolm waited, that knot in his stomach grew. It was like there were two shoelaces. One was the worry about Aggy—alone and cold out there, maybe even hurt. And the other was Malcolm's lie. His breaking of the Academy bylaws. In short: his rattiness. These two laces snarled and grew and tightened inside him until Malcolm couldn't sleep. He couldn't sip his antibacterial water. He couldn't even nosh or nibble.

Have you ever had someone suspect you of the worst, Mr. Binney? It's a hard, heavy thing. And the heaviest part was Malcolm had no idea what to do about it. All he could

do was wait. He couldn't even nibble his whiskers. They were already stubs.

Monday morning came and Amelia bounced in. She set a heavy book on their table. "Malcolm! I brought you something! Look, it's a dictionary." Her dark eyes shone.

Malcolm could barely lift his head and squeak a greeting. Still no word from the Academy. Surely, if they had found Aggy, she would tell them what had happened, right? That of all the dumb things Malcolm had done, hurting Aggy hadn't been one of them. But the Academy's silence must mean they hadn't found Aggy. Or worse—maybe they had, but they hadn't found her fast enough.

Amelia frowned and tapped on Malcolm's cage. "Malcolm? What's wrong?"

Malcolm didn't know how to begin to answer. But he didn't have to. Because then you came in, Mr. Binney. And in spite of his own feelings, Malcolm's ears pricked up. No offense, Mr. Binney, but you were positively disheveled.[32] Your hair stuck up not only in the back, but all over. And you looked like you hadn't slept all weekend either. Even Jovahn stopped flicking chunks of playground mud at Amelia. "Whoa, Mr. Binney."

You ran your hand through your hair and took a rattled breath. "Jovahn. Class. Good morning. You know, I've been thinking."

The class inhaled all at once—I mean, we had never seen you so frazzled before, Mr. Binney. We were imagining the worst: The principal had outlawed recess for fifth-graders for the rest of the school year, maybe. Or you were going to be fired because our math test scores were so abysmal.[33] Maybe even that your house was hit by a meteor and you were now radioactive.

"It's time we cleaned our desks."

"Aw, man!" You probably couldn't tell our relief with all the groaning.

You held up your hands. "I know, I know. But we've got a lot of special events coming up. Parent-teacher conferences, kindergarten buddies, and the Dedication Day car-

---

[32] Disheveled = untidy, unruly. It's kind of the opposite of Amelia. Nothing about her bag or locker is ever disheveled. Vocabulary from 10/4.

[33] Abysmal = horrible. As it turns out, our math test scores *were* abysmal. Guess we do need those morning warm-ups. Vocabulary from 10/13.

nival. As fifth-graders, we are the leaders and role models for all of those. And we want to be fifth-graders who are organized and take pride in our building, right? Well, it all starts with the inside of your desks."

Around the room, desk lids creaked open. Soon the room looked like the meteor had hit it instead of your house. Crumpled-up spelling tests, sticky granola bar wrappers, and broken crayons massed on the floor and tabletops. Skylar found his missing retainer (in Michael's lunch box). Tianna got mad at Kiera all over again by re-reading six weeks' worth of notes.

Meanwhile, you were cleaning out your desk, too, Mr. Binney—dumping drawers and sifting through confiscated slingshots (Jovahn's) and paper footballs (Skylar's).

Amelia had nothing to do during this time, since technically, she didn't have a desk and she was already a role model of organization. So she bit her lip—and wondered. "Mr. Binney, are we looking for something in particular?"

You hesitated. "Yes. Please, class, if you come across something that isn't yours—other than Skylar's retainer—please bring it up here. I'm missing a small blue box. It's velvet and square and about this big." He held his hands up and made a shape with his thumbs and forefingers about the size of two of Skylar's paper footballs put together.

Now Malcolm's ears really perked up. Malcolm knew that box. It was the one you were always peeking into after school, Mr. Binney. But you had just had it . . . when was that? Thursday? After school?

Kiera's ears perked up, too. "Velvet? You mean, like a jewelry box?"

Was that a flush on your cheeks, Mr. Binney? "Well, yes, Kiera. Now, about those notes."

Meanwhile, the rest of the class started cleaning again with renewed vigor. After all, it is much more exciting to search for something than to sort old worksheets into the recycling bin.

But Amelia hadn't asked only for your sake, Mr. Binney. No, now that the class was distracted, Amelia pulled out her hair elastic and scooped Malcolm out of his cage. She cracked open the dictionary and plopped Malcolm on it. "Tell me, Malcolm. Tell me what's wrong."

Malcolm guiltily thought of her unread note. How to explain? He sniffed the dictionary. This book, as thick as Malcolm was tall, seemed to be all words. Well, most books are, I guess, but this one wasn't a story, it was *about* words. Lists and lists of words. Any word Malcolm could want. Any word Malcolm could *need*.

Slowly, Malcolm extended a foot. *Saturday.* He pawed through a few pages. *Pet. Disappear.*

And before Malcolm knew it, he was dancing over the pages. Tapping, pointing, flicking, poking, stamping. The whole story. Everything. The Midnight Academy. Aggy. The lie. The note. And most of all, how Aggy was gone now and how no one knew where and how everyone thought it was his fault. Oh, it felt good. Telling Amelia felt as good as a quality burp that eases an overnoshed stomach.

Malcolm finished and stared up at Amelia. He panted. His feet were slick with sweat.[34]

Throughout it all, Amelia had been quiet. Simply listening. Have you ever known a person like that, Mr. Binney? Someone who just listens? Someone who doesn't interrupt or pipe in with their opinion or wince at your dumb mistakes? Anyway, it's one of the most wonderful and satisfying things to have. And Amelia listening like that made Malcolm Know. Know with a capital *K*. No matter what Honey Bunny said, no matter the rules of the Midnight Academy, Malcolm hadn't been wrong; Amelia *was* his friend. And if you can't tell your friends things—things that are making you feel as tangled up inside as a kindergartner's shoelace—well, then, what good are friends?

Malcolm got a sip of water. Then Amelia broke off a piece of graham cracker for him and finally spoke. "Well, I know you're not asking me what to do, but if you care to know, it's quite simple, really. You've got to find out for yourself where Aggy is and what happened."

Malcolm put down the graham. Amelia had spoken the very thing he most longed to do—help Aggy. But what could an undersized rat do?

Amelia leaned closer and continued, "Don't you see?

---

[34] Yes, rats sweat through their feet. If you think about it, it's not any stranger than sweating through your armpits.

That's the only way for the Academy to believe you—about any of it. Sure, you could wait here and maybe they'd figure it out, but you'd still be a rat who lied. And what if they don't find her? You'll always be under suspicion."

Malcolm considered. He stretched out his paw. *What. If. I. No. Find?*

Amelia shrugged. "You won't be any worse off then, will you?" She settled into her chair, her eyes gleaming. "Now. You must have some ideas about what happened."

Malcolm nibbled the graham. He had had a lot of time to think over the weekend. And all he could think about was that cat with the dusty, dry voice and the deadly breath to match it. Snip. How Aggy had hissed at her. How she had refused to come to the floor where Aggy was. How Aggy—even Honey Bunny—had said she was up to something. Was taking Aggy it? Or was there more?

A shout made Amelia and Malcolm jump.

"Hey, Mr. Binney, is this it?" Jovahn asked, pointing to a bookshelf near Malcolm's cage. Tucked at the back, on top of a row of books, was a small blue box. The small blue box you had opened and closed so many times before and after school.

"Yes!" You strode over to the shelf in two steps, Mr. Binney. "How'd it get over there? Thanks, Jovahn. Good eyes. Okay, the rest of you, two-minute warning. Finish up and be ready for math."

You scooped the box up, Mr. Binney, but before you

101

shoved it in your pocket, you couldn't help peeking in it. You'd done it so many times before. Only this time, you stopped in your tracks. And your mouth fell open. Malcolm didn't know why at the time, but I know you do, Mr. Binney. And again, for the sake of the story—Malcolm's story and what happens later on—I'll write it here.

The box was empty.

CHAPTER 12
A SPY FROM ABOVE

That night, as Malcolm listened to the beep and click of Ms. Brumble locking McKenna's doors and leaving, he wasn't at all sure that Amelia's idea was a good one. For starters, what exactly—besides a three-foot green lizard with orange bouncy ball–shaped eyes—should he even be looking for?

Nevertheless, Malcolm let himself out of his cage and snuck under the door. Because, as Amelia also had said, what did he have to lose?

Malcolm skirted the shadows of the hall. He slowly made his way to the stairs, the same stairs he had come tumbling down a few nights before. Snip seemed like the place to start—the Academy certainly seemed to think so. Hadn't Honey Bunny accused Malcolm of working with Snip?

But how do you spy on a cat if you are a rat? A smaller than average rat?

Malcolm hunched at the bottom of the stairs. If he marched up them, he'd be Snip's midnight snack faster than Jovahn could inhale a bag of cheese curls. But what other way was there?

Brrriiinnnnggg!

Malcolm jumped. Of course! With Aggy missing, the Academy would be meeting more often to discuss things. Maybe Malcolm could learn something from them. He scurried up a row of lockers. His Knack couldn't help noticing the orange cutout letters on the black bulletin board across from him, next to the library: MCKENNA'S DEDICATION DAY CARNIVAL!

Malcolm slowed. He had heard so much about this back in Room 11, but it still wasn't exactly clear.[35] "Celebrate the 90th anniversary of McKenna's historic clock tower," he read. "Food! Games! Halloween costumes optional. 1–3 p.m., October 29." Malcolm squinted at the pictures. Nutters running. Playing. Nibbling. Crumb, too bad the Dedication Day carnival wasn't for critters. It looked like something a rat could really twist his tail around.

But there was no time for daydreaming about Nosh

---

[35] In fact, he had intended to ask Aggy about it, but then, well, you know.

and Fodder, even if it came in the form of caramel popcorn and decorated goodie bags. The Academy was coming.

Thump, thump, thump.

Pitter-pat. Pitter-pat.[36]

Malcolm shrank in the shadows atop the lockers, and he followed the sounds of the critters, out of sight, out of scent. Honey Bunny thought Malcolm was a sneaky rat spy? Well, Malcolm would show him.

"Do you think they're okay?" That was Billy. Malcolm recognized her whisper.

Honey Bunny grunted a reply that Malcolm couldn't make out.

Harriet grumbled, "I still prefer the old way."

The critters went right past the library. Maybe they weren't meeting. But where were they going? Malcolm hesitated at the library door. Should he continue to follow? Or maybe, while the Academy was somewhere else, it was the perfect time for Malcolm to check out the library. He remembered the Academy notebook and the computer where Octavius took notes. If he could find and read them, maybe this all would make more sense to him. Maybe he could explain himself better.

Malcolm slipped through the transom, then down a bookshelf and over to the library counter.

He had taken about two steps when a splash of water jolted him.

---

[36] Sadly, no *scritch . . . scritch . . . scritch* from Aggy.

Oscar! He had forgotten all about Oscar!

Malcolm skitter-skattered and bonked straight into the computer monitor. As he shook his head to get his bearings, he noticed that Oscar was nosing in his gravel. Gristle, was he going to report Malcolm to the Academy? Malcolm hadn't even found anything out yet!

"Hey! Hey, I didn't do it," Malcolm waved his front paws and whispered through the glass. "Oscar, I didn't do what the others think. I don't know where Aggy is. I'm not working with Snip."

Oscar studied him for a moment, his fins fanning. Then he went back to nudging the gravel. Malcolm closed his eyes, dragged some valor up from deep within, and peered at the words.

"DUH."

Malcolm gazed at the fish with eyes as wide as a nutter whose teacher just announced that the pop quiz wouldn't be graded. He let out a deep breath. "What?"

Oscar nudged the beads again. "DUH."

Malcolm sat back. "You believe me? But—why?" Wasn't Oscar the fish who had tried to eat him his first night of the Academy?

The fish stuck his snout in the bottom of the aquarium. Malcolm watched, then read, "NOT A RAT."

"Oh," Malcolm said, his hopes crumpling. He stood and took a step backwards. "Oh, but—that *is* true. I *am* a rat."

Oscar blew a string of bubbles out of his mouth. Malcolm wasn't sure how to tell with fish, but he got the

feeling that this one was getting impatient with him. Oscar added some beads. "WE THINK YOU NOT A RAT."

Malcolm didn't know what else to say. He *was* a rat. That was about the only thing he truly knew in this whole mess. But he also didn't want to argue with the one critter who believed him.

Oscar sat gaping at him a moment, opening and closing his mouth, spouting a trail of bubbles.

Scrape, scrape. Someone was coming!

Malcolm darted this way and that. Where to hide? Where to hide! Another splash from the aquarium got him to look in the water again.

With a flick of his tail, Oscar had wiped the last sentence away. Now he swept a fin across a different line of letters—"LOCKER 2135 UP"—and waved his right fin toward the door.

Huh?

But there was no time to ask or even get to the door. Instead, Malcolm leaped up a bookcase and then over to the long row of fluorescent lights that hung across the ceiling of the library. He carefully stepped around a stranded paper airplane.

Far below him, the Academy gathered on the library computer. Guess they were meeting after all. Malcolm watched as Octavius flipped on the computer.

Then the phone rang. Honey Bunny knocked it off its cradle. Pete banged his pincher on a button on the keypad, and Tank the turtle's voice filled the room. "Hello?"

"It works! The cell phone works!" Jesse did a flip with glee. "I told you. Welcome to the twenty-first century." He high-pawed Billy.

Harriet sniffed. Honey Bunny asked, "Polly, are you there?"

A high-pitched, airy voice chirped. "I'm here. Flying right above Tank. The phone rubber-banded to Tank's back works brilliantly. Jesse, you're a genius."

"What do you see?" Pete asked in his accented voice.

"Well, we made it up to the Fourth. We're heading into the old science lab room." A pause. Malcolm supposed that there might be a few long waits if they were going at Tank's speed. After a moment, Polly whistled. "Whew, what a mess! Someone's been busy up here."

"Remember when the lankies did that asbestos[37] removal on the third floor two years ago? Does it look like that?" Harriet asked.

Another pause and some static. "I don't know . . . maybe."

"Any signs of Aggy?" The Midnight Academy members leaned closer to the phone's speaker.

Tank spoke. "No. There was a scent on the stairs, but nothing since then. But there's junk dribbled all over in here. Let's see if I can sniff it out."[38] Another pause. "Strange. It's . . . paste. And the Grumble of the Brumble's lemon cleanser."

---

[37] Asbestos. Not a vocabulary word, but according to Malcolm's *New Webster's Student Dictionary,* it's a substance used in buildings a long time ago for insulations and fireproofing. Unfortunately, it also causes cancer.

[38] Box turtles have a very keen sense of smell. Nearly as good as a rat's.

"Look!" Polly cried. "The second-graders' missing hand sanitizer!" And louder, "Watch out, Tank! Don't step in that." There was a bump and a rattle, like Tank had banged against something. Then Polly came back on. "The chemicals from the storage cabinet have spilled, too. Tank, let's get out of here. The fumes are making me all confuddled."

"Okay. Hang on." There was a long pause. Were Tank and Polly going to go all around the fourth floor? At this rate, the conference call would take all night.

Then a squawk from the phone. "Hey, what's this?" The Midnight Academy all leaned in. So did Malcolm. The row of lights tilted. Just a little. But it was enough. Next to him, the paper airplane slid toward the edge.

Gristle! Malcolm dove for it. But the plane dropped off the edge of the light, out of reach. And now it was Malcolm who was falling. He twisted and caught himself just in time. His sweaty front paws made tiny squeaky noises as he slowed himself on the curved surface of the light. His back end pedaled furiously in thin air.

Meanwhile, Polly's voice floated up. "We've got critter tracks!"

Malcolm watched helplessly while the airplane glided through the air and zoomed toward the library counter as the Academy asked, "Aggy's?" Malcolm held his breath.

"No, they look like—"

There was a small splash from the aquarium. The plane landed safely in the shadows behind the Academy. Malcolm let out his breath.

"They're rat prints, aren't they?" Honey Bunny interrupted. He sounded tired.

"Maybe," Tank said. "It's hard to tell. Polly's going ahead, scouting it out."

"He lured her up there." Honey Bunny started pacing. "But why? And where did the rat take her?"

Malcolm cringed as he reached with a rear paw to get back onto the light. Honey Bunny was talking about *him*.

Billy spoke up. Her voice wasn't loud, but it was steady. "What if we're wrong, HB? What if Malcolm didn't have anything to do with this? Those tracks could have been from the other night when he went up the elevator."

Jesse nodded. "He seems like a good critter." Malcolm felt a pang of friendship for the hamsters.

"Are you crazy?" Honey Bunny bellowed so loudly that Malcolm jumped.

And it was that little movement that did it. What weak grip Malcolm had on the light suddenly was gone.

Squeeeeaaak! He slid down the side of the light. Then he cartwheeled through the air. As he did he heard Honey Bunny saying, "He's a *rat*. Snip has found her rat fink this time."

Then he landed. It didn't hurt. It was a soft landing. That's about the only good thing you could say about it. Otherwise, it was absolutely the worst place a rat could land.

Malcolm had fallen squarely on the fluffy, banana-chip-scented head—of Honey Bunny. "Oof!"

"Lankies!" Harriet the hedgehog shrilled and wheezed. "Sour Grapes!—Sour Grapes!—this is not a drill!"

The critters scattered—hopping, scooting, jumping in every direction.

Honey Bunny bucked Malcolm off. His eyes widened at the sight of him. "You," he growled. Then he roared, "Freeze!" The other animals stopped in midbound.[39] "It's not Sour Grapes." Honey Bunny pointed with his paw. "It's Skuzzy Rat."

---

[39] Way better than the fifth-graders do when you say it, Mr. Binney. Really, I know you've taught for years, but you might want to observe Honey Bunny in action.

Malcolm huddled on the counter, his tail wrapped tightly around his body, his short whiskers drooping. He opened his mouth to say something—anything!

But absolutely nothing came out.

Pete scuttled back to the counter. He reached out his pinchers and pain zinged through Malcolm's tail. "I'll take care of this," said the hermit crab.

And so it was—for the second time that week—that Malcolm was escorted back to his cage via hermit crab. And, as Malcolm nursed his tail, he knew that all he had done was convince the Academy that he was, indeed, a rat fink. A rat fink who had no merit whatsoever when it came down to sneaking and spying. A rat fink with a very tender tail.

CHAPTER 13

LOCKER 2135 UP

"You can't let that get you down," Amelia said the next day. It had taken her nearly fifteen minutes to unwind the sandwich bag twist ties that the Academy had used to secure Malcolm's cage. "That was an accident. It could have happened to anyone."

Malcolm locked his coffee-black eyes with Amelia's. She tried to squash a smile. "Well, okay, maybe not *anyone.* But it still wasn't your fault."

Amelia continued, "Now, more than ever, you need to find out what happened to Aggy. If they all think it's you, well, then they're looking in the wrong direction. They'll never find her."

Malcolm wished he had Amelia's conviction.[40] It was

---

[40] Conviction = a strong belief in something. Honey Bunny always spoke with conviction. Vocabulary from 9/17.

like how getting your homework done first thing after school sounds good during the school day, but gets so complicated outside the classroom. Malcolm let out a tiny sigh and took another bite of cinnamon Pop-Tart. Amelia was right about one thing: He owed it to Aggy. She had believed in Malcolm, too.

So that night, Malcolm made his way out of Room 11 again. This time he was looking for a locker. Amelia had already scouted it out. It was down on the first floor, across from the art room and the old girls' gym.

2131, 2132, 2133, 2134 . . . 2135. Malcolm sat back on his haunches and peered up. The locker looked like any other locker.

Or did it? Malcolm stretched up on his hind legs. This locker's bottom vents were bent and warped—from one too many kicks, maybe. Whatever the reason, it was big enough for an undersized rat to squeak through. Malcolm wiggled. His hind end stuck for a moment (too much peanut butter?), then he was through. His right leg caught a little and Malcolm found himself falling with a thud to the bottom of the locker.

It was dark inside. Dark and smelly. Malcolm's nose wrinkled at the old gym clothes that he had fallen into. He vehemently[41] hoped that he hadn't landed in what nutters called "underwear."

Malcolm untangled himself and found himself crunch-

---

[41] Vehemently = with passion. Amelia vehemently wished Jovahn would keep his shoes on. Vocabulary from 10/21.

ing atop an old Doritos bag. What was so special about this locker, anyway? It was as messy as the insides of Skylar's desk.[42]

Malcolm snuffled in a pile of old math worksheets. But wait now—something thick and heavy was tucked under there. Malcolm flipped back the papers. They whirled around and he ducked and covered his ears (rat ears are very tender when it comes to paper cuts). When the papers settled, what Malcolm saw caused the first grin to spread on his face since he had been banished from the Midnight Academy.

It was a cell phone. With the words "Property of V. Brumble, Clearwater School District" etched on the side of it.

Malcolm had found the phone that Jesse had stolen. But if Tank and Polly had been using it last night, what was it doing here? And then Malcolm saw on the side of the locker:

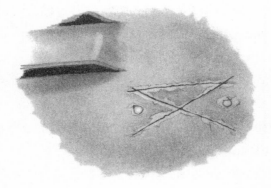

---

[42] AKA: The Pit of No Return. It would surprise no one if Skylar found underwear in his desk.

This was an Academy Niche. A safe spot. Complete with the Grumble of the Brumble's stolen cell phone. Tank and Polly must have made it back all right last night then. Malcolm breathed a sigh of relief.

Of course, a Niche is only safe if you are on the same team as the Academy. Malcolm knew that. Was this some kind of trap, or did Oscar want Malcolm to find the Niche and the phone?

And then Malcolm remembered: "WE THINK YOU NOT A RAT." The "rat" part aside for a moment. Who was *we*? Could it be that Jesse and Billy were trying to help him, too? Or Polly and Tank? Had they left him the phone?

As Malcolm pondered this, he noticed something else. A pipe. A pipe the width of a jump rope handle running up the length of the locker. Not every critter could scale it, but a rat is meant for climbing.

"UP." How far did it go?

Only one way to find out. Malcolm sucked in his stomach and scuttled up the pipe.

Malcolm climbed through the floor of the third floor and into a girls' bathroom. Clearly not used in some time. And still the pipe continued. Malcolm took a deep breath and followed the pipe through to the fourth floor.

Here, Malcolm peeked out around the pipe. Not a locker, not a bathroom. Malcolm was in a radiator heating vent. And from what he could see, it was the same radiator heating vent he had listened to Aggy, Honey Bunny, Jesse, and Billy through the last time he had been up here. Only now, he was under it, in a space so small that even if a cat was lurking, she would never be able to reach.

In other words, it was perfect. A perfect way to get up to the fourth floor without anyone (such as a violent, hoarse cat) knowing.

As Malcolm silently thanked Oscar, he peered out. Dark, except for the glow of the exit signs. Malcolm would have to rely on his nose. He wished again that his whiskers were longer. Why did he always chew them down right before he really needed them?

Malcolm crept out. Now where would he find a cat up

here? And for the first time, Malcolm wondered, *why* was a cat up here? Where had Snip come from? Did she ever go out?

Yes, this was the Fourth, all right. Even if Malcolm didn't recognize the radiator, he'd know the dusty, chalky, stale air. The jumble of old school furniture. Desks, chairs, filing cabinets, old computers—it was the perfect obstacle course for a rat. Or a cat.

Malcolm eased out under a table, edging along the underside of it. Across the hall from him was a room. If his rat sense of direction was accurate, it was directly above the library on the second floor and Aggy's room on the first floor.

Malcolm crept through the door. It was a classroom at one time. High ceilings stretched above him, with two rusty ceiling fans at the top. The wall of windows must have at one time flooded the room with light, but now two were boarded over, and another was cracked. All of them were streaked with grime. The moonlight barely penetrated through the glass.

Long, scarred black tables stretched across the room, their surfaces coated in dust. In between the tables were taller counters with deep black sinks in the middle. Malcolm crept closer. His pink nose jiggled like mad. Gas. Chemicals. Malcolm knew this scent. It was the smell of science![43]

---

[43] Just the regular smell of science. Not like that one time that Skylar tripped and shattered the jar of mothballs.

Through the dim light, Malcolm saw boxes of hand sanitizer, lemon cleanser, and an open jar of paste, identical to the one in the kindergarten room. Just like Polly and Tank had described. Polly had been right about the smell, too. Malcolm's head swam as he carefully avoided the puddles on the floor.

No sign of Aggy or the cat, though. But there were fresh scrapes in the dust on the floor where something had been dragged or pushed.

Malcolm's ears swiveled at the sound of a slight rustle under the cracked window. "Aggy?" he whispered. He wondered if cats or iguanas had a keener sense of hearing. He figured he'd soon find out.

Then—from the hallway—footsteps! Malcolm glanced around. He clamored up a bookcase.

A light bounced around in the hall. Who could it be? It was well after midnight by now and besides, this floor was closed. Whoever it was shuffled through the mess out in the hall. There was a soft thump, then, "Ow!"

The flashlight beam pierced the darkness of the science room. A tall shadow—definitely a lanky—navigated the tables and crept to the boarded-up window. The lanky poked around—looking on shelves and in drawers and even the garbage can. The lanky slowly ran the light along the edge of the floor and wall, then the windowsills. With a flash, the beam hit the window and reflected light onto the lanky's face.

Mr. Binney! What were you doing there?

There was a radiator in the room, too. Under the cracked window. You sat on it[44] and ran your hands through your hair. You pulled out a Granny Smith apple. After staring at it a minute, you took a bite and reached into your shirt pocket. Out came the little blue box—that jewelry box. You flipped it open. From Malcolm's vantage point above you, he could see what he didn't know before.

Yes, the box was still empty.

Now, Malcolm was fairly sure you hadn't spent all this time staring at an empty box. And it was pretty clear that you were looking for something up here. So he had to assume that what you were looking for was supposed to be in the box. What he didn't understand was why. But it was clear from the state of your rumpled hair that it was important.

You took another bite of your apple and sighed before snapping the box shut and tucking it away.

"Mark! What are you doing here?"

Malcolm's head whipped around. Ms. Brumble stood in the door, her own flashlight in hand. What the cheese? The school was supposed to be empty this time of night, but so far, it had been busier than the drinking fountain after gym class.

You jumped too. "Ronnie! You scared me!"

She crossed the room and flashed her light around.

---

[44] Don't feel too bad that you didn't smell and notice what Malcolm and Tank could. Human noses are about as sensitive as a bunch of boys around a crying girl.

"Geez, what a mess," she muttered. Then she aimed the light at you. "No, really. What are you doing here?"

You patted your shirt pocket. "Um, well, remember when I was up here helping you move this stuff around the other night? I think I left something. My—my flashlight. See? I found it." You hopped up. "We can probably go. But what are *you* doing here?"

Ms. Brumble frowned.[45] "I was leaving for the night and heard that noise again. That—shriek."

You grinned, Mr. Binney. "You mean the ghost of McKenna?"

Ms. Brumble snorted. "No, I think someone's been up here. All this stuff has been moved and spilled. And look—" She pointed. "Another window's cracked." She put her hand on the radiator. "And the heat's on." She sat down on the radiator, pulled your apple away, and bit into it. "I wish I could lay my hands on the kid breaking all these windows. Do you know that the kindergarten room window was broken and their iguana is missing? I tell you, I'm not sure those pets are worth it. When they're not making a mess, they're breaking kids' hearts."

Malcolm's own heart panged at the mention of Aggy.

You sat back down beside her. "Oh, I don't know. I think the kids need to learn to take care of something. And sometimes a pet is the only friend they've got."

---

[45] For the record, you are a terrible liar, Mr. Binney. There is no way that Ms. Brumble bought that. The fact that she didn't question it just shows how soft she is on you. Or are we kids not supposed to know about that?

"Yes, but if something happens . . . remember the third-graders last year when their mouse or whatever ran away? I had a kitten when I was a girl. When I lost it, oh, I was devastated."

You squeezed her hand, then slid to the floor. "C'mon. It's going to be an early morning."

You were about to leave when a cry pierced the room. Not a scream from inside the room, but from somewhere nearby and above the room. Gristle! Malcolm ducked. The ghost of McKenna!

Then something solid and heavy and very un-ghostlike hit Malcolm. Hit him so hard, he flew off the shelf and landed with a thud and burst of dust on the table—right in front of your shocked faces.

Do you remember the night you saw the rat on the fourth floor, Mr. Binney?

Didn't know it was your own pet mouse, did you?

CHAPTER 14
A DEAL WITH A CAT

Yeeeeoow! The black shadow—yes, it was Snip—leaped down to the table. Malcolm dodged the long claws. He darted and fell into an empty sink.

You saved his life, Mr. Binney. "What in the world?" You flashed your light over toward Malcolm and Snip. Snip was caught in the beam. From below, in the sink, Malcolm could see the matted black fur with ribs poking through, the too-tight collar cinched into the cat's neck. And also, the bared, pointed teeth. She hissed at you. But it gave Malcolm enough time to scurry out of the sink and get a head start up some cabinets on the back wall.

Snip yowled again. And chased.

"Shoo!" Ms. Brumble shouted. Mr. Binney grabbed her

hand, pulling her to the door. "C'mon, Ronnie, let's get out of here!"

Ms. Brumble pulled back. "I should do something, Mark. I'm the school custodian!"

You yanked harder. "Tomorrow, Ronnie. In the light."

And with that, the two of you ducked out of the room. (Not that Malcolm blamed you, Mr. Binney. He was doing his best to get the crumb out of there, too.)

Malcolm, meanwhile, tore up to the top of the cabinet. But from there, there was nowhere else to go. And Snip's wheezy breath was right behind him. It smelled of chemicals, like the back of the room. Malcolm was trapped.

Now Snip took her time. Despite her mangy appearance, she slipped up through the shadows of the room like she belonged to them.

At the top of the cabinet, Malcolm dashed back and forth, looking for an escape. But the only thing near him was the ceiling fan. The ceiling fan! The blades hung nearly ten feet out from the cabinet. Could he make it? Malcolm didn't have a choice.

He leaped.

Malcolm landed on the edge of one of the fan blades. It rocked and spun slowly. For a second, Malcolm thought he was going to crash to the floor like he had the night before. (Only without the soft Honey Bunny landing.) Then his rat claws caught hold and he heaved himself over the edge of the blade.

Wow, what a leap! Malcolm bet no mouse or rabbit or sniffy hedgehog could ever do that.

Of course, a cat probably could. Malcolm looked across at Snip. She was pacing on the top of the cabinet now, where Malcolm had been, her white-tipped tail weaving, weaving. Would she jump?

Then the fan jolted. Malcolm looked up. His little rat weight had pulled it out of the ceiling some. No way could it hold Snip, too. If she leaped, they'd crash to the floor.

Malcolm looked down. Could *he* jump? Directly below him was a sink filled with a murky liquid. A hose drained the sludge from the sink to a bucket. The odor was so strong, Malcolm could taste the chemical tang from it. His head swam and suddenly he knew exactly what Polly meant by "confuddled." He couldn't fall into that.

Snip must have guessed his thoughts because she sat down on top of the cabinet and said, "No, I don't recommend jumping into my brew, mouse. No telling what might happen." Her voice was raspy and hoarse. At the end of each sentence, she sucked in air. "Or should I call you 'rat'?"

Malcolm stared. He was scared speechless, to be honest, like Amelia is when she has to give her oral book reports. The only thing that calmed him down was the thought of Aggy. After all, this had been his whole point of coming up here—to find Snip.

Malcolm cleared his throat. "Where's Aggy?"

Snip laughed, if you could call the windy heave from her throat a laugh. "Well, you're to the point anyway. You mean that lizard? That little club of pets downstairs thinks you made her vanish, don't they? And now you're going to prove them wrong?"

How did she know all that? And furthermore—did she just call him a *rat*?

She must have seen the astonishment in Malcolm's face. "Oh, yes. I know." She huffed. "I know. That pampered pet club that says they're the eyes and ears and whiskers of the school? They don't know anything. *I* know. I *know*. All the secrets of McKenna. All the secrets of the Midnight Academy." She raised her furry eyebrows. "Oh, yes. Secrets. They didn't tell you about that, did they? They've got you thinking they're some noble organization with a heroic history, don't they?" She snorted, a huffing sound. "I could tell you stories that would make your fur fall out."

Malcolm's stomach churned. He wanted to say, "Like what?" Instead, he said, "So you know about Aggy? Where is she?" Malcolm's eyes kept going to Snip's tail. That white tip was winding around and around in a slow figure eight. It was hard to look away.

The cat hacked and wheezed. "If I did, why would I tell you?"

Malcolm pulled his gaze from the tail. Rats can't see colors very well, but he noticed her eyes glowed in the dark—wide orbs that seemed to suck him in. Malcolm said the first thing that came into his head. Something he often overhead Jovahn say. "Maybe I could help you. You tell me what you know. About Aggy or about—about the Academy."

Snip cackled. "You? Help? Me? With *what?*" This last word got caught in her throat. She coughed.

Malcolm didn't know. What would Snip want that he had?

Snip continued coughing, clearing her throat. She pawed at the light blue collar, so tight on her neck. Malcolm snapped to attention. The collar. He *could* help, he knew. Of course, it would put him in immediate danger. But if he could figure out a way . . .

"Your collar," he said. "It bothers you, doesn't it?"

Snip lowered her paw slowly. Her tail stopped moving, and she fixed her glowing eyes on him.

Malcolm took that as an indication she was listening. "I could help with that collar. You know, rats are great gnawers. Amelia—a friend of mine—told me once that rats' front teeth grow up to five inches in a year. My teeth are ready. I could snip that collar in seconds." Malcolm took a deep breath. The more he talked the more valorous he felt. "If you'd want."

Snip continued to stare. Her front paw raised and brushed the collar. That was when Malcolm knew he had her. He had put his tail on the very thing Snip wanted most but couldn't do herself.

She took a rattling breath. "What would you want from me?"

"What you know about Aggy."

Snip laughed that rough sound again. "And what if it was me? What if I've got her? Isn't that what you think? Isn't that why you're up here?"

"Then I want to know where. And why." Malcolm swallowed. "We both know I'm not working with you. I need proof I can take back to the Academy."

Snip paced the top of the cabinet. "When? Where?"

Malcolm had already been thinking of this. He'd need a place where he could still be undercover. Where Snip couldn't slice him up as soon as he snapped the collar. "The radiator. You know the one. I'll meet you there tomorrow night. At—at midnight. I'll be under the radiator and you can lie down with your back to me. After you tell me what you know, I'll gnaw your collar."

"Ah, clever rat. Or you think you are, anyway. Yes, I'll meet you tomorrow night." She stretched and jumped from the top of the cabinet. She landed on the bookcase near the door. Her tail curled around the light switch. "Provided you survive until then." With a flick of her tail she flipped the switch and leaped out of the room into the darkness of the hall.

The fan! She had turned it on. As Malcolm started spinning, he could feel himself being pulled to the outer edge of the fan blade. He dug his claws in. But he knew he couldn't hold on for long. The fan's motor roared, faster and faster.

Malcolm looked around the room for a soft place to land, to jump to. But everything was a blur, whizzing by. Malcolm's stomach heaved. He closed his eyes. His claws plowed through the painted metal of the fan blade. He was on the edge now. And the blades were still picking up speed.

Why had he thought he could out-trick Snip? She was probably already waiting below. Waiting for him to fall. Then she'd pounce on him before he could even get his balance.

The fan whirred. "I'm sorry, Aggy!" Malcolm cried as his claws finally lost their grip. He felt himself flying through the air, arcing through the dusty space high above the tables. He had been going so fast, his last thought as he let go was that it wasn't Snip who was going to kill him. When he hit the wall, the impact would.

Only it didn't. Because he kept on sailing through the air. By sheer luck, he flew over the tables, over the radiator, and right out the cracked window.

CHAPTER 15
OUTSIDE

The night air was much cooler than inside the school. The smell of wet leaves and rain wrapped around Malcolm as he hurtled toward the ground. Crazy thoughts crashed through his head: Would he ever see Amelia again? Would he ever nosh again? Would it hurt more to land on the pavement or the sidewalk?

It was neither. Malcolm's fall was broken by one of those pokey-looking shrubs outside our classroom window. Its branches slashed at him as he fell through it. And by the time he stopped, his nose (deeply scratched) was about three inches from the white gravel underneath the bush.

Malcolm took a long, quivering breath and jumped to the ground. The school's outside lights sliced through the dark like a dirty look from Kiera. Malcolm sniffed. He hadn't been outside like this in—well, *ever*.

What would you do if you found yourself in a place you'd never been before? Would you hunker down and watch at first? Or would you sprint out and start exploring? Do you know Malcolm well enough yet to know what he did? Let me give you a hint: There was no peanut butter involved. Malcolm stayed put. Just until he could figure out how to get back in.

He was peering out at a small parking lot. Only one row for cars, empty now, of course. Across from the parking lot was another bank of boxy, overgrown shrubs with chalky gravel underneath. Over them, a huge, glowing orb hung in the sky. Why did the moon look so much bigger outside than from inside in a cage? A breeze blew through— a thick, damp wind that ruffled the wet leaves on the ground. Fall would turn into winter soon. Malcolm had heard someone say that that morning. But he had never known the weather changes he'd heard so much about. He was an inside pet. Malcolm's nose twitched. He gnawed on a whisker.

The breeze shifted. Malcolm rose up on his hind legs. What was *that*? The aroma of Nosh and Fodder wafted across his sore pink nose. He stepped out of the bush's shadows.

Malcolm scooted along the edge of the curb until a giant metal box on wheels loomed over him. It was huge, as tall as a lanky; as wide as a free-throw court. The rich, thick smell oozed from the box. It seemed like every scrap, nubbin, crumb, morsel, speck, shred, swill, and driblet Malcolm had ever tasted, sniffed, or dreamed about was in that box. Malcolm trotted around it, his nose wiggling furiously.

You know how you always say that the ten minutes before lunch are useless, Mr. Binney? Because we're too hungry to think? Well, Snip could have come up and tapped Malcolm on the shoulder and he wouldn't have even noticed. He was a rat on a mission. A one-snack mind.

There had to be an opening. Malcolm put his front paws on the metal, found a groove, and crawled up. The top of the metal box was two rubber flaps. And inside those flaps? Garbage! Paper scraps, wrappers, old milk cartons, leftover applesauce, bits of crackers, pineapple tidbits, grilled-cheese crusts.

Do you know where Malcolm was? Yes, his nose was deep in the cafeteria dumpster.

Malcolm's stomach squeezed in happy anticipation. What luck! He'd feast, then, once he was properly fueled, he'd figure out how to get back inside.

Where to start? Malcolm pawed at the pile, turning over a soda can. He took a sniff—was that peanut butter? He licked it so clean the pop top came off. He was all set to throw it over his shoulder when—

"Oooh, can I have it?" A nasally voice behind him made Malcolm jump.

Malcolm spun around and came face to face with—a rat. This rat was a proper rat, though. Beefy. Glossy. With a tail as strong as a tetherball rope and a body as long as Jovahn's supersized sneakers.

The rat snatched the pop top out of Malcolm's stunned paws. He threaded the pop top on his tail, where two others already rested. He held his tail out to admire. "I love the glim. Isn't it dazzly?"

The rat circled Malcolm slowly. "You're a new rat out here, right? I'm Clyde."

Malcolm spun around, trying to follow Clyde, but succeeded only in getting his hind leg stuck in a yogurt

container. He kicked it off just in time to hide the end of his tail in his front paws. Gristle, why were his whiskers so stubby, so puny? He really *had* to quit chewing them—but hey, hold on. Malcolm croaked, "Did you—how did you know I was a rat?"

The rat stopped and looked at him exactly like you eyed Skylar the time he asked if he should put his name on his social studies test, Mr. Binney. "Well, because you *are* one? What else would you be? You're no Chihuahua." Clyde tipped his head and considered. "Did you hit your head in that fall?"

Clyde *knew* Malcolm was a rat. Clyde knew Malcolm was a *rat*. You can't know how that felt. Have you ever gone your whole life with people thinking you were one thing, but knowing deep inside that you were really something else entirely? And Clyde saw through that. Saw right through to what Malcolm really, truly was. And it didn't disgust him.

Malcolm felt a little like dancing.

Instead, he said, "Yes. I mean, *no*. I mean—yes, I'm new. And no, I didn't hit my head. Just—just my nose. And my whiskers." Might as well blame them on the fall.

Clyde picked up the yogurt container. "So, where are you from?" he asked, licking at the rim.

Malcolm pointed. "Inside."

Clyde pulled his head out of the container. "Inside? You mean, like inside the school?"

Malcolm nodded again. He crept toward a half-eaten breakfast burrito.

"Oh, man! You lucky rat! You made it out! Wait until you meet the others. They aren't going to believe this! Come on, I'll take you." Clyde scampered to the edge of the dumpster, the pop tabs on his tail clinking.

Malcolm hesitated. Go with Clyde? Others? Everything was moving so fast. He needed to get back inside, right? He couldn't stay out here. Could he?

Staying out here would be easier. No Midnight Academy. No Honey Bunny. Out here, he could be a rat. A *rat*.

Malcolm glanced up at the looming brick side of McKenna. But inside was Amelia. Aggy. His Comf-E-Cube. And Room 11. There it was—Malcolm recognized the poster of *Despereaux* the mouse through the window.

Malcolm also noticed something else. A drainpipe snaked up the side of the building, past four floors of ivy-covered windows. But most important, it went right past Room 11's far left window, and that window was open a crack. We already know how Malcolm can slip through the smallest of spaces. In other words, it was a way back in.

If Malcolm wanted it.

Clyde sensed Malcolm's hesitation. "What're you waiting for?" Clyde's eyes followed Malcolm's stare. "Oh, no. Oh, curdled crumbs! You're not thinking of returning, are you?" Clyde edged away at the thought of it. "They're going to put you back in a cage, you know. You'll have the

smaller ones poking at you every day, pulling your tail—
it's awful."

"No, it's not like that," Malcolm started. How could he
explain? Everything he knew was inside. And out here,
yes, he'd be a rat. But he'd be just a rat. A dirty rat, maybe.
Or a rat fink, even. Never a rat of valor. Or of merit.

"I—I need to."

Clyde shook his head. "You're fermented."

Suddenly a shriek echoed through the night. The same
one that had brought Ms. Brumble up to the fourth floor
earlier that night. It was the same one that Malcolm had
heard inside, right before Snip had pounced on him. Only
out here, the scream came from high above. It bounced
around off the walls.

Malcolm had never lived in the wild, but instincts told
him to take cover.

Clyde dove into the shrubs.

And Malcolm dove off the dumpster and into the ivy.

CHAPTER 16
THE LUMMOX MAKES A GUESS

"Oh, Malcolm. Look at your nose!"

Malcolm blinked awake. Sunlight poured in through the windows. The classroom bustled. Amelia peered down at him. What time was it?

He stretched. From the looks of the classroom activity, it was after lunch already. Quiet work time. He touched his tender nose and stepped onto Amelia's offered hand.

She rubbed her nose on his. Malcolm's insides turned as quivery as the leftover yogurt from the dumpster the night before. Yes, coming back was the right thing to do.

"How did it go last night?" Amelia asked in a whisper as she set him down on the dictionary.

Malcolm stretched again, then started looking for the words on the page. So much to say. For the first time, he wished he had a voice that nutters could understand.

Amelia, as usual, listened carefully. Her eyes grew wide at Malcolm's description of the locker. Her hands clenched at Snip's taunting. Then, "She flung you out the window?" Her voice rose to outside levels.

Next to them, Jovahn tilted back in his chair, a book propped on his stomach. Amelia scowled and put a finger on Malcolm's paw. She waited for Jovahn to tip back up. But he didn't. She pressed her lips together. "Hold on," she whispered. "I have an idea."

With one quick move, she scooped up Malcolm. Then a stretch of her arms—and Malcolm was stuffed in the hood of her sweatshirt. She grabbed a book and walked to the front of the room, where she snatched the library pass and stepped out into the hall.

Crumb. Amelia was *good*.

Malcolm peeked out once and spied Oscar, who splashed a subtle greeting.

Amelia kept going, all the way to the back corner of the library. There, behind the tall rows of shelves, she opened a book and said quietly, "Malcolm, can you hear me? Squeak if you can."

Malcolm peeped out. He glanced left and right. Except for a model skeleton leering down at them from the top shelf, no one else was in sight. Amelia had found a place where they could talk privately—have a real conversation.

Her own little Niche. He squeaked softly and climbed to Amelia's shoulder. Her strawberry shampoo had his knees weak. From there, he jumped to the bookshelf. Now they were eye to eye.

But before Malcolm could begin to explain, a nutter stepped into the aisle. Malcolm shrank into the shadows behind the books.

Jovahn. Jovahn?!

"Amelia, you're supposed to come back."

Amelia stepped in front of Malcolm's hiding place and

casually pulled a book off the shelf. "Okay, I'm almost done."

"Uh, I think he meant right away. There's a quiz. He's all grumped up. Something else is missing from his desk. He thinks somebody's stealing stuff in our room. Me, I think it's Kiera. Did you see how excited she was about his jewelry box?"

Amelia didn't answer. She put the book back and pulled out another one. She studied the back cover. She wound a strand of hair around a finger.

Jovahn waited. Then he kicked the bottom of the book-shelf. Finally, he sighed. "Okay, it's your detention." He slipped away.

Amelia peered behind the books. "Malcolm, you okay? Whew, I thought that lummox would never leave! Here, get back in my hood and I'll show you—"

"Gotcha!" Jovahn bounded around the corner. Amelia jumped. The book in her hand fell to the floor. Malcolm dove into the depths of Amelia's hood. Jovahn pointed at her. "Who are you talking to?"

Amelia scowled and picked the book up. "What? I'm not talking. It's called reading aloud, you numb-brain."

Jovahn stepped closer. "No, you weren't. I was listening." He looked up at the top shelf, scanning. "You were talking to someone. And you called him 'Malcolm.'" A grin flashed across his face.[46] "I know what's going on here."

---

[46] You know the grin, Mr. Binney—like before he booby-trapped your wastepaper basket?

142

Amelia sniffed. "You're crazy. I don't know what you are talking about. But if you don't mind, I'd like to check out a book, so I can get back to the classroom." She reached around Jovahn and pulled a book off the shelf.

"On Lamborghinis?" Jovahn raised his eyebrows. Then his grin faded. "You know," he said, "I won't tell. He's here, isn't he? Our mouse?"

Amelia wheeled on Jovahn so fast that Malcolm fell over in her hood, his stomach lurching. "Like I'd tell you. And for your information, he's not a mouse!"

Deep in Amelia's hood, Malcolm covered his eyes with his paws. Across the library, Malcolm heard Oscar splash.

Jovahn frowned. "Huh?"

Amelia flushed. She opened her mouth once. Then she grabbed a book and stomped off to the checkout counter.

Malcolm crawled to the top of Amelia's hood to peek out. He watched as Jovahn sighed and followed Amelia out of the library. He looked so . . . dejected, shuffling his feet behind Amelia. Malcolm wanted to squeak up. But he was hearing the echo of the Academy's rules: *Never communicate with humans.*

Then, as they entered Room 11, Jovahn raised his eyes. And they met Malcolm's coffee-black ones.

It wasn't communicating. Not exactly.

But Jovahn grinned again.

And Malcolm was left to wonder: Was it any less critterwise to have two nutter friends?

CHAPTER 17
BLACKBERRY

It was ten minutes to midnight by the time Malcolm headed upstairs.

Yes, Malcolm had decided to meet with Snip to clip her collar. If he truly wanted to find out about Aggy, what other choice did he have? But Malcolm shook so badly his remaining whiskers vibrated.

As soon as he poked his head up from under the radiator, Snip was there, pacing. "So you survived the fall? I should have known. You rats are virtually indestructible. Living on garbage, nesting in holes, like those rats outside. That's why you've survived so long as a species."

Malcolm drew a deep breath. "Do you want your collar off or not?" His voice boomed a little in the radiator. It sounded so unlike how he was feeling.

"Say I do." Snip crouched and crawled closer. Malcolm could see the glow of her eyes, level with his own. He smelled the dusty, chemical scent of her breath. He was careful to stay a paw's length back from the edge of the radiator.

Malcolm gulped. "Then I need to know something. Where's Aggy?"

Snip wheezed. "That lizard? I'd love to have done something to her—in a much bloodier way. But I didn't."

"Where is she?"

Snip shrugged. "What do you care? That Academy is a bunch of corrupt, lazy critters, only out for their own good. They did you a favor by kicking you out." She laid her head on the floor, her back to Malcolm. "Now, your side of the bargain. Come on, be a good rat."

Malcolm started toward her, then stopped. "But you haven't answered my question. I asked where she was."

Snip rolled over. She hacked out a laugh. "You are a tenacious[47] one! What makes you think I know? Or that I'd tell?"

"Didn't you tell me last time that you know everything that goes on in our building?"

Snip leaped to her feet with a snarl. She paced. She hissed.

Malcolm pressed his mouth shut and stayed silent. Snip unconsciously pawed at her too-tight collar.

---

[47] It would seem that over the years, Snip listened in on some vocabulary lessons, too. It wasn't one of Room 11's words, but just so we're clear: tenacious = stubborn. Jovahn was tenacious in his attempts to catch Amelia and Malcolm together.

She arched her back, her fur spiking high. "All right! All right. Check the clock tower. That's all I'm going to say. You'll see. Now gnaw!" Her last words were low and so forceful that Malcolm obeyed without even thinking about it.

He sank his teeth into the collar. It was leather, and it was old and brittle. It was so tight, no hair grew around it.

Snip flinched as Malcolm gnawed, but didn't move away. "At last," she purred. It sounded like sandpaper. "Oh!" She yelped as Malcolm nipped her skin a little.

"Sorry." The collar was so tight! It was a wonder Snip could even speak. "Why—how did you get this on?"

"It was put on me when I was a kitten." She hissed. "I grew. It didn't."

"But—" He drew back. "You're a pet?" Malcolm suppressed a shudder at the thought.

"Just gnaw!" she said. "And the collar, not me!" But after a minute, she spoke again. "You'll find out. Those smallish creatures—what do you pets call them?— *nutters?* They don't really love you. I had one once. She dressed me up, tied bows on my tail, carried me everywhere. She even brought me to McKenna for the Dedication Day carnival— do you know about that yet? Everyone in the courtyard, running around in costumes, laughing, eating, drinking. She dressed as a witch. I was her black cat, hidden under her cape. Until they spied me. Locked me inside the school office. 'It's too disruptive to have a kitten outside, dear. Your kitty will be fine here.' Only she never came back for me. The school grew dark; people went home. And I was still there. I was there for days." Snip cleared her throat with a noise that sounded a lot like thirty chairs scraping across a tile floor. "Then I stopped crying. And when the door opened on Monday morning, I ran."

Malcolm paused. "Your nutter didn't come to look for you?"

"Just finish, rat!" Snip growled. "And no. She didn't. She was off having fun with the other creatures. Didn't give me a thought."

Part of Malcolm didn't blame her. If Snip was anything like she was now, he wouldn't have come looking for her either.

One last nibble and the collar sprang off Snip's neck with a snap.

And as it did, Snip whirled around. She slashed her extra-long claws through the space under the radiator.

Yeow! Malcolm jerked backwards, slamming his head into the pipe. He wasn't fast enough. Snip's claws ripped through his left ear. He rolled away, to the far back corner. Blood gushed down. He couldn't see. He couldn't smell. But he could hear. He could hear Snip, clearing her throat and yowling. It echoed the throb of pain in his ear.

"Come out, you rat!"

Malcolm's head swirled. Around him, the world faded. His last thoughts were wondering, Had Snip done that on purpose? Talked so much to distract him?

Then everything went dark.

When Malcolm woke up, he thought he had been blinded. Then he realized that the blood from his ear had dried his eye shut. He set to grooming. He was still sore, but now he could at least see. He peered out from under the radiator. The dust swirled around in the daylit hallway. He couldn't believe how different the fourth floor looked in the light. Almost safe.

But—daylight! What time was it? Malcolm listened. The building was still silent. School hadn't started yet. But, judging from the sunlight, he'd have to hurry before the lankies started arriving.

Malcolm was all set to dash down the pipe when he noticed Snip's collar curled next to him. Light blue leather, about the width of a pencil. It looked like at one time it had rhinestones on it, though all the stones were missing now. Only the tiny prongs were left, poking out in little spikes. The collar was so old the buckle had fused together.

Malcolm nudged it with his nose. Hanging from the buckle was a silver disk. He had seen these before. They were name tags. You could get them engraved at the Pet Emporium for $4.99.

Malcolm pawed the tag over. The writing was almost worn away. *Blackberry*, it said. *I belong to Veronica: 555-9762.*

At one time, Snip *had* been a pet. Was the rest of her story true?

At the last minute, Malcolm hooked the collar with his tail and carried it with him down to Room 11.

CHAPTER 18
LOST, THEN FOUND

Amelia stared at the collar. "So, Snip was a pet named Blackberry?"

They were inside the girls' bathroom. After Jovahn's nosiness from the day before, Amelia wasn't taking any chances. ("Let's see you snoop around and follow us here, neanderthal.")

Malcolm shrugged. It seemed inconceivable[48] to him, too. Someone owning Snip? Someone loving Snip? And if she was a pet, what had happened? Why would the little girl leave Snip at school and never come back for her?

"Hmm," Amelia said, fingering the collar. "I wonder . . ."

Uh-oh. Malcolm knew that look.

---

[48] Inconceivable = impossible to comprehend. Vocabulary from 11/17. Amelia found it inconceivable that Jovahn could be trusted.

And before Malcolm could dart away, he was back in Amelia's hooded sweatshirt (green to match her green socks and green hair elastic).

And when Malcolm peeked out, they were at locker 2135.

"Malcolm," Amelia whispered, pulling him out of her hood. "The phone. Do you think you can get it out? Because if you can, we could call."

The number, to find out about Snip! Malcolm leaped from Amelia's hand.

Inside the locker, he hefted the phone up (it turns out that phones, even the smallest of them, are tricky for rats to move). It barely fit through the bottom warped vent.

Amelia scooped it up along with Malcolm. She slipped back to the bathroom and locked herself in a stall.

She set Malcolm on the toilet paper roll. "Now, let's find out what's going on!" As Amelia punched the number from the collar into the phone, she muttered, "If my mom would get me a phone of my own, we wouldn't have to go through all this." She sighed. "Shhh! It's ringing! Hello? May I speak with Veronica please?"

There was a pause. "Oh, is she in school then?"

A longer pause. "Oh! Well—" Amelia touched the worn leather of the collar. "Well, we found her cat, Blackberry."

"What?" Amelia frowned. "But I—well, no. The cat's not actually here." A long wait, in which the collar slipped from Amelia's fingers to the floor with a jangle. Then in a rushed voice, she said, "Yes, of course, you must be right. Sorry to have bothered you." Amelia clicked the phone off. She stood there, lost in thought.

Malcolm waited a moment. Then he squeaked.

Amelia stirred. She picked up Malcolm and set him on her shoulder again. "You're not going to believe this," she said, unlocking the stall door. "It was a woman who answered. Older. She said—well, first she said that Veronica hadn't lived there in years. Then when I mentioned Blackberry—Snip—well, the woman went all quiet. She said that Veronica had a cat named Blackberry when she was in fifth grade, but it disappeared. Ran off when Veronica broke her ankle at the Dedication Day carnival at McKenna." Her eyes grew wide.

Hold on a whisker. Malcolm's brain was whirring faster than a tail-safe wheel.

"She said Veronica cried more about her lost Blackberry than her broken ankle."

Malcolm thought back to last week and all the commotion when Tianna sprained her wrist on the playground. Could a tiny kitten have been left behind in the confusion of an accident?

But Amelia wasn't done yet. "Malcolm," she said.

"There's something else." She picked him up and swallowed. "She said that was a long time ago, almost twenty years." She swallowed. "How can that be?"

They stared at each other.

Then the bathroom door burst open.

Malcolm squeaked and dove into Amelia's hood. "Oh!" Amelia squawked. The phone dropped from her hand and skittered across the floor.

It came to rest at the feet of . . . the Grumble of the Brumble.

All three of them stared at it.

"Hey! I've been looking everywhere for this." Ms. Brumble set a roll of toilet paper back down on her cart and picked up the phone. She squinted at Amelia.

Oh, scrap. How in nubbins was Amelia going to explain how she had Ms. Brumble's phone? She wasn't even supposed to be on this side of the building, much less using a staff member's property. The whole thing was probably a suspendable offense—whatever that was. Definitely not "being the fifth-grader you wanted to be" behavior.

Amelia gulped, clearly thinking the same thing. She opened her mouth. No sound came out at first. "Um, we—I found it. Here in the bathroom."

Ms. Brumble studied Amelia. She pursed her lips. "Really. Well, where was it?"

Amelia tried to squeeze around toward the door. "Um, on the shelf . . . under some papers. You know . . ." She waved vaguely.

"Uh-huh." Ms. Brumble turned the phone over, examining it. Then her eyebrow ring jerked down at the screen. "How—what's that doing on here?" she said under her breath.

Amelia opened the door. "I'd better get back now. You know Mr. Binney—"

At your name, Ms. Brumble's head came up. "I do." She glanced back at the phone. Then she shook her head and pressed a button on it. She put her hand on Amelia's arm. "You're Amelia, right?"

Oh, double scrap!

Amelia nodded stiffly.

"I've heard about you." Ms. Brumble seemed to be trying not to smile. "I'm sure Mr. Binney's missing you." She bit her lip, then leaned in and whispered, "And his mouse." She patted Amelia's hood.

Amelia froze. Malcolm burrowed frantically.

Ms. Brumble laughed. "Relax. Mr. Binney's told me what kind of fifth-grader you are." She waggled the phone in her hand. "You've saved me a lot of grief. I was dreading reporting this missing. But I think you both better scamper back to where you belong."

Deep in the hood, Malcolm's mouth fell open.

Ms. Brumble slipped the phone in her pocket and picked up the toilet paper roll again. "Go on, then. And stay there," she ordered. "Mr. Binney doesn't need to deal with a loose pet."

154

CHAPTER 19
THE ONE UNFORGIVABLE PET ACT

Malcolm and Amelia scurried out of there faster than Ms. Brumble could imagine. Partly because they didn't want her to change her mind. But mostly because there was a number echoing in their heads.

Twenty years? Had Snip been up on the fourth floor for twenty years? How long do cats live, anyway?

"Imagine," Amelia said, "being up there, all alone, all those years."

A few days ago, Amelia had written out the alphabet on a page in her notebook. It took longer, but it was less noticeable than Malcolm dancing through the dictionary. Malcolm tapped across the letters, spelling out, "Maybe find out more when go to clock tower tonight."

"What?" Amelia said out loud. Jovahn jerked around

in his seat. Amelia glared, then scribbled, "Malcolm, you can't go. Don't you see? This is getting dangerous! First your nose, then your ear, and now—well, you can't."

Malcolm stared. Hold on a whisker. Didn't Amelia sneak Malcolm out of Room 11 and use a stolen cell phone? And then lie about it?

No, Malcolm wasn't the only one doing something dangerous. And wasn't Aggy still missing? Of course he was going. It was the only thing he had left he could do.

Malcolm spelled slower. "I have to."

"No!" Amelia smacked her hand on the notebook. Malcolm bounced on the table with the force of it. "Who knows what that thing is up there? The ghost of McKenna, maybe!"

"What are you doing?"

Jovahn stood on the other side of the table, his mouth full of granola bar. Malcolm's nose twitched. Almond.

How long had Jovahn been standing there? What had he seen? Amelia slammed the notebook shut, scooped up Malcolm, and turned her back on Jovahn.

Jovahn swallowed his bite. "No, seriously," he said coming around the edge of the table. "You *are* talking to him. And it almost looked like—"

Kiera whipped around in her seat.[49] "What?" she said. "Amelia's talking to mice?"[50]

---

[49] It really wasn't all that loud. Kiera has supersonic hearing when it comes to gossip.

[50] This was much, much louder. Intentionally louder, so that everyone within earshot would look. Which was the whole room.

Jovahn took another bite of granola bar and stepped closer. "Yes. And the mouse—"

Amelia flushed a deep pink. "Jovahn, shut up!" she growled through her teeth.

Kiera stood up. Jovahn blinked.[51] "He was pointing out—"

Malcolm's claws dug into Amelia's hand. Surely Jovahn wouldn't say it? But if he did, if Kiera heard, everyone would know. And if everyone knew—well, this was probably why the Academy had rules like *no communicating with humans.* Everything would change. It wasn't critter-wise.

Malcolm had to do something! He wiggled frantically in Amelia's hand. Jovahn opened his mouth. "He was—"

Malcolm did the only thing he could think of. He committed the One Unforgivable Pet Act: He sank his long front teeth (these were very ratlike if any had ever cared to check) deep into Amelia's thumb.

"Ow!" Amelia yelped.

Malcolm jumped to the floor. Had it worked?

"He bit her!" Kiera screeched. "Malcolm bit Amelia! The mouse bit Amelia!" she repeated, even louder.

---

[51] There should be some scientific research done on how lip gloss glare deadens boys' common sense.

Yes, it had worked. Kiera had forgotten all about what Jovahn had been about to say.

Malcolm hunched near Amelia's shoe. The room loomed huge above him. Huge and silent. Malcolm wasn't sure he'd ever before heard complete silence in Room 11. Now it was aimed at one thing: a little red spot welling on Amelia's thumb.

"He bit you," Jovahn said.

"He *bit* me," Amelia whispered. Malcolm shrank under the computer table.

Kiera's shouts and the silence had gotten your attention, Mr. Binney. You strode to Amelia's side. "Let me see." You frowned. "Go down to the office and have them wash it out," you said. "Jovahn, walk her down."

Once Amelia and Jovahn left, the silence, the eyes, shifted.

To Malcolm.

He cowered under the table. You bent down and stuck your hand out, Mr. Binney. Your face seemed as big as the moon. "Come on, little guy."

Now what? The bite had changed everything. Malcolm could sense that, even without whiskers. Malcolm knew all about pets and biting. Animals were often brought back at the Pet Emporium for it.

"He bit my son!" the mom would huff. "We can't have a pet that bites. It's too dangerous!" And the poor, confused dog, cat, hamster, guinea pig, bird, you-fill-in-the-blank, would be back in the Pet Emporium. Or worse. Sometimes, the pets didn't return to their cage. Sometimes, they went in the back room and they never came out again.

But Malcolm didn't have a choice about biting. Malcolm had to stop Jovahn from saying something. He *had* to.

Malcolm knew one thing: If he was caught by you, Mr. Binney, he wasn't going to be free to wander at night. He probably wouldn't even be at McKenna ever again. And leaving McKenna meant Malcolm would never learn what happened to Aggy. He'd never prove the Academy wrong. He'd never be a rat of valor and merit. He'd be a rat fink— worse, a rat fink who bit.

So he had to do it, Mr. Binney. It probably didn't look like valor and merit from where you crouched on the floor, swearing under your breath. But sometimes doing the right thing and being the fifth-grader you want to be takes some surprising turns.

Malcolm took a deep breath. He trembled. And—he ran.

You said a word under your breath that had gotten Skylar sent to the office last week. Malcolm sprinted across the classroom. He aimed for the door. No clinging to the edges. Straight across. Nutters screeched. Some even pulled their feet up on their chair.

It hurt a little, seeing how the nutters were scared of him.

But Malcolm didn't have time to ponder it.

Because you were after him, Mr. Binney.

CHAPTER 20
FLUSHED

Malcolm skittered out into the hall. Unfortunately, the fourth-graders were coming in from gym class. He dodged stomping sneakers and dribbling soccer balls, and narrowly missed getting swept off his feet by a girl dragging her jacket on the floor.

You followed Malcolm out into the hall, Mr. Binney. You chased in that funny half-run, half-walk teachers do when there's an emergency but they don't want to alert the students to it.[52] Malcolm was down the hall and almost around the corner before the shrieking started. It was some silly fourth-grader. "Mouse! Mouse! MICE!"

---

[52] No offense, Mr. Binney, but you didn't stand a chance against Malcolm, running like that. And it makes your hair flap.

In less than a second, the entire hall erupted in shouts. Some kids ran screaming away from Malcolm, clinging to their lockers. Others (you know the type, Mr. Binney) dove at him. Malcolm wheeled and leaped and twisted like he was avoiding Jovahn's Dodge Balls of Death.

He skidded around the corner, bouncing into a metal garbage can with a *bong*.

Luckily, this hall was empty. A few kids peered around the corner, but for the most part, their involvement only slowed you down, Mr. Binney. Malcolm raced for the end of the hall. If he could get down the stairs, maybe he could make it to the Lost and Found. The Niche. Malcolm could hide in there.

"Stop!" you half shouted. "Stop that mouse!"

And out of nowhere, a long-handled broom shot out of a doorway. Ms. Brumble. A stealth attack. Malcolm hadn't noticed her cart in the hallway.

The big, fuzzy broom head slammed to the floor in front of Malcolm. A near miss. Malcolm coughed at the cloud of dust that puffed out from the broom. *Slam!* Again the broom narrowly missed Malcolm.

"Don't hurt him!" you shouted, Mr. Binney. "It's our class pet."

"What?" Ms. Brumble switched tactics. She pushed with her broom, scooting Malcolm along on the floor. She grumbled under her breath, "I don't know what I was thinking, transferring here last year. I could have had Fairfax School! It's pet free. And I wouldn't have to set up tents in a courtyard for some blasted Dedication Day carnival thing." Malcolm zigged and zagged, looking for a way out. You and Ms. Brumble closed in. Malcolm scurried down the row of lockers. Mr. Binney, you put your foot out to stop him. Malcolm went right over your shoe, on the outside of your pant leg, and darted under a door.

It was the bathroom—the same one he and Amelia had been in. Malcolm ran to the farthest corner and hid behind a toilet.

But you were right behind him. The bathroom door flew open.

"We'll find him, don't worry," Ms. Brumble said, bending low. She poked and prodded with her broom. "Did that girl let him out? I told her—"

"What? No." You moved the garbage can, rifling through the paper towels, and groaned. "It's a long story, Ronnie. Where could he have gone?"

You two were looking on the floor, so Malcolm climbed up. He scaled the toilet and jumped on the toilet paper roll. If he could hide until the dismissal bell rang, you'd have to go back, then, Mr. Binney, right? You wouldn't leave the nutters alone, would you?

But you two lankies weren't giving up easily. You opened the first stall door with a bang
that shuddered the toilet paper roll Malcolm
crouched on. It started spinning. Malcolm
jogged to keep up.

Bam! That was the next door. The roll
spun faster. Malcolm ran faster. Gristle, this
was like his tail-safe wheel, only he was on
the outside of it and there was no way to get
off!

Bam! Malcolm panted, barely keeping up. Layers
of toilet paper spooled onto the floor.

Bam!

"He's here!" You and Malcolm locked eyes.

Malcolm froze. The momentum of the toilet paper roll flipped him over and around. He landed with a lurch on the toilet seat. But those seats are slippery.

And you know what happens next, don't you, Mr. Binney? How could you forget? I mean, it's not every day that you corner a rat you think is a mouse who has bitten one of your students and is probably going to cost you a very long conversation with her parents, not to mention the principal. And it's been a really long day and how is it possible that you've lost so many things of importance lately?

To your credit, you did reach out. But Ms. Brumble barged in and also tried to scoop Malcolm,[53] and the two of you tangled and wedged in the narrow stall door.

Let's face it, neither of you has the reflexes of a rat. Only lankies.

Splash.

---

[53] Malcolm wants to acknowledge these acts of valor and merit.

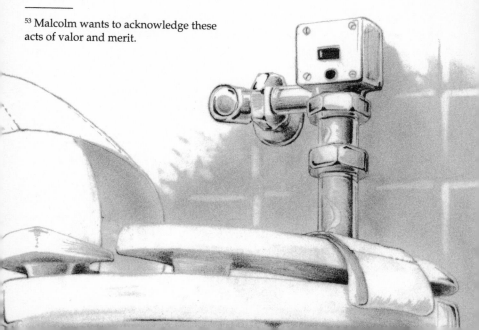

And before you or Ms. Brumble or Malcolm could do anything but wrinkle your noses, a roar rose in the room.

The automatic flush.

Malcolm swirled once, twice. He reached out to you. But the pull of the water was too strong.

The last thing he saw was the look of horror on your face, Mr. Binney. And Ms. Brumble, putting her hand on your shoulder.

CHAPTER 21
NOT A RAT

That look. That look in your eyes, Mr. Binney.

It hurt.

I know, the look was probably because you were seeing a critter being flushed down the toilet, but to Malcolm it was much more than that. Your look was the final crushing blow. He felt like that time Kiera pulled the chair out from under Skylar and he sprawled on the floor in front of everyone. Here Malcolm had thought he was a beloved pet, but instead he was another problem. A dirty rat.

Down and down he went, taking bends and battering his sore head and ear and nose and tail along the way. Each curve in the pipe seemed to bang open a memory of his rattiness. His lie about the mouse-rat business. Aggy's disappearance. Rat fink. The Academy shrinking away from him in the kindergarten room. The nutters' screams as he escaped. And finally, Amelia's shocked whisper, *"He bit me."*

Let's face it, if you looked in Amelia's encyclopedia or dictionary, Malcolm swirling through the skuzzy pipes of McKenna would be the exact opposite of valor or merit.

The crooked pipe shot him out into a larger one. Malcolm tried to gulp a bit of air before getting tugged down again. Even as he gasped for breath, he wondered, What was the point? Everything he wanted was gone. He'd messed it all up, in the Academy and in the classroom. And now, with every second, he zoomed farther and farther away from it.

But . . . hold on a whisker.

What *was* the point?

Why *had* he bothered to take a breath back there when the pipe split?

Why, when all hope and air and bacteria-free water were gone, when he was the sneaky, lying, dirty, stealing, biting, skuzzy rat fink that everyone warned that he'd be, when he had been flushed down a *toilet*, for crumb's sake—why did he take a breath? Not everyone would.

But Malcolm had.

And Malcolm remembered something.

Honey Bunny, talking that night in the kindergarten room. *"You don't know rats. It's all about survival for them. They'll do whatever it takes to get their next meal, their next breath. They're cunning, sly creatures. Not to be trusted."*

And Snip: *"You rats are virtually indestructible. That's why you've survived so long as a species."*

Malcolm's mind careened out of control, like Skylar on a field trip with too much Mountain Dew in him. What if all the bad stuff—being exiled from the Academy, running away from Room 11, getting flushed—*had* happened because of his rattiness?

But what if his rattiness was what could get him *out* of all of it, too?

Malcolm dragged his claws on the next bend, slowing slightly. Snip and Honey Bunny had spit out those comments as if those were bad things, but maybe they weren't. Not entirely. I mean, "doing whatever it takes" in the right light is determination and perseverance, isn't it? And cunning—well, isn't that really being clever and smart about solving problems? And survival certainly isn't anything to sneeze at, no matter what kind of critter you are.

The water rushed around Malcolm, over his head and his ratty ears and tail and stubby whiskers.

And then it hit him straight in his ratty face: Maybe Malcolm should stop trying to avoid being the rat everyone thought he was. Maybe he should stop trying to become the rat he thought he should be. Instead, maybe Malcolm should be the rat he *was*. His true self—who he was when no one else was looking.[54]

Malcolm shot out all four of his paws, twisted his body, and wedged himself from going any farther down the pipe.

Was *that* what Oscar had meant when he had spelled out "NOT A RAT"? Maybe Oscar hadn't meant what species Malcolm was; maybe Oscar meant what kind of critter he was. You know, *inside*.

Yawning up in front of him was a wide grate. Malcolm knew from a recent report by Jovahn exactly how the city plumbing worked.[55] He couldn't get sucked into the sewer. He was a survivor, after all. A survivor rat who would do anything to get what he wanted. And what he wanted was here in McKenna. Room 11, Amelia, the Midnight Academy's respect—and Aggy.

Malcolm turned, and he swam. He didn't even know he could swim. But he rat-paddled like no rat ever had before.

---

[54] Like, for example, at midnight.

[55] Remember his actual flushing model? How he sent the Raisinettes down? You have to admit, Jovahn may have his own Knack.

And slowly, inch by inch, he moved backwards against the current. And when he reached a Y in the pipe, he ducked into the calmer water. And he kept swimming. The water grew shallower and shallower, until finally Malcolm came to a drain. He barely had the strength to pop the drain cover. He poked his head out into a dim, hot, rust-smelling room.

Where in nubbins was he?

Malcolm sank back down, letting the drain cover settle over him. Tired. Wet. Cold. He curled up into a ratty little ball. And after a few minutes, he drifted off to sleep.

It was exhausting being the rat that he was.

CHAPTER 22
A MEETING IN THE BOILER ROOM

Malcolm woke at midnight with a headache and a stomachache. The headache from all the knocks in the pipe. The stomachache because he was starving. Do you realize that Malcolm had never had to find his own food before? Ever. From the sawdusty pellets at the Pet Emporium to the buffet of treats in Room 11, Malcolm had always been fed. But now he would have to start scavenging. Like a real rat.

Malcolm uncurled his body and poked his head out of the drain cover. He sniffed around. The room was about as big as Room 11, except the floor was crumbling cement and the walls were tile. In one corner, a monstrous metal box—as big as your Toyota, Mr. Binney—rumbled and roared. Farther back, a huge round tank burped and hissed. Both were laced and woven together in a crazy jumble of pipes and ducts that twisted and turned and angled all around the room before they disappeared through the walls and ceiling. It reminded Malcolm a little of what he had learned about hearts and veins and arteries in our circulatory system unit. He wasn't positive about what was being pumped around McKenna—heat? water? peanut butter? —but it was clear that this room was the heart of it all.[56]

Malcolm's feet started to sweat. First, because of the heat of the room. But also because—well, those pipes! It was a giant maze waiting for him to explore. A rat amusement park, if you will. Malcolm wished Jesse James and Billy the Kid were there. How they'd love this place.

But no. Focus. Nosh first. Then—well, where would he go? Not back to Room 11, that was for certain. Malcolm pushed the thought out of his head and focused on his stomach.

He was about to slip out into the hallway when his slashed ear twitched. A whirring—familiar somehow.

Malcolm scrambled to a hiding place behind the Toyota-sized monster. It roared to life as he ducked under it.

Suddenly, a spear of light pierced the room as the door opened.

Malcolm watched the wall for shadows. But there were none. The ghost of McKenna?

No, critters. Malcolm couldn't see them, but he heard them. Two voices. One, a soft mutter he couldn't quite

---

[56] Do you know where Malcolm was, Mr. Binney? Have you explored that floor of McKenna, too?

make out. The other, a hissing, hacking noise that ended in a cough. Snip. But what was she doing down here?

"It's ready," Snip rasped. "I've moved it down here for the big day. Do you know how long I've dreamed about stepping out of the shadows and finally biting back? I want to slash my claws and leave a mark on those hideous creatures they call nutters."

The second voice said something. Malcolm strained, but he couldn't catch the low tones over the roaring of the monster above him. What was ready? And who was she talking to? Malcolm raced to the other side. But the jungle of pipes blocked Malcolm from seeing anybody else.

Snip spit something out of her mouth, saying, "Yes, here it is. Ah-ah-ah—" She slipped a paw over it. "Not so fast. It's yours, once you keep the Academy out of the way. All you need to do is watch. The tall creatures will go up to set the clock. And when they leave the building, *you* make the call. And then—splashy, splashy!" She wheezed out a laugh that ended in a coughing fit.

A faint clinking sound, another murmur. Malcolm raced back to the other side. He could hear better there.

"Don't be greedy. It shouldn't be hard. The Academy's already chasing after that pathetic pet rat. But when they finally find that scaly leader of theirs? Well, let's just say that'll keep them . . . occupied."

Malcolm shivered. Pathetic pet rat—that was him. Scaly leader? That must be Aggy!

But the rest?

In truth, Snip made about as much sense as Jovahn does when he babbles on and on about the different levels of his video games. All Malcolm knew was that something bad was going to happen.

Something to the nutters. And something to Aggy. But when? And what?

Out in the hall, a soft *thump*. Malcolm's ears swiveled.

"Go!" hissed Snip, and the two critters scurried toward the door. Malcolm crept behind them. He had to know who was with Snip! He squeaked through the heavy door before it slammed shut.

Malcolm blinked in the dim light of the hallway. It was narrow, damp, and cold, without any of the once fancy woodwork or glazed tiles of the upper floors. It reminded Malcolm of the back of the Pet Emporium.

It was also empty. Snip and whoever had been with her had vanished.

Malcolm glanced behind him. "Boiler Room," he read on the door. He wasn't sure at all what a boiler room was, but nevertheless, he thought he should know. So he put the boiler room into the rat map system of his brain. Then he started looking for a way out.

Malcolm bobbed his head right and left, so his nose and what remained of his whiskers could warn him of anything coming up. He turned the corner. What was this? His nose tingled.

An open metal sliding door. Of course, the whirring sound! The elevator.

To a lanky, the elevator was its usual grimy, empty box. But to a rat—well, Malcolm's nose was as twitchy as a nutter before spring break. He breathed in deeply and his head swam in confuddlement. That tang, that chemical mixture . . . science! This was the same smell from the science room on the Fourth. Malcolm remembered—what had Snip called it?—the brew in the sink. Had Snip brought it downstairs?

Then Malcolm caught a whiff of a third smell. He stooped lower. He even pawed a little with his claws to make sure. Yes, it was undeniable.

Banana chips.

There was only one critter he knew who noshed on banana chips.

Oh, scrap.

Suddenly, everything clicked into place. Honey Bunny! The other critter with Snip!

"You'll have what you want," Snip had hissed. And Honey Bunny did—he had control of the Midnight Academy. Without Aggy, he was their leader. And it couldn't be more obvious that Honey Bunny longed to be in charge. How many times had Malcolm heard Honey Bunny gripe about Aggy being too soft?

Malcolm sucked in his breath, remembering Honey Bunny's bandaged leg the night of Aggy's disappearance! Could Honey Bunny have gotten cut on the window by breaking it himself? And then Malcolm and his lie had happened along at just the right time! Malcolm's rattiness was the perfect thing to pin this all on. No wonder Honey Bunny was so eager to jump all over him. It was to cover his own big, rabbity tracks!

The realization made Malcolm shrink against the wall. He drew a sign in the dust on the floor.

But he couldn't "get out—fast," as much as he wanted to. He had to stop Snip and Honey Bunny. Before it was too late for Aggy. Or the nutters. Because if he didn't, who else would? Not the Academy. Thanks to him, the lying, skuzzy rat, not only would they not believe him, but they were looking in all the wrong places.

He eyed the elevator. Better to leave it where it was. The only advantage Malcolm had was that Snip and Honey Bunny didn't know that he knew. (Whatever it was that he knew.) Malcolm's head felt as snarled up as when you do those brainteasers in class, Mr. Binney.

Malcolm *did* need to go up. But how? He didn't relish going back the way he came down. Besides, he wasn't sure he had it in him. He was all rat-paddled out.

No, there was only one other way Malcolm knew to get back upstairs.

He eased down the hall. Hopefully, if the elevator was there, then . . . yes! A rusty double door with a warped bottom. Warped enough that a draft of air blew under it. A draft of wet leaves and moonlight.

Outside.

Once outside, Malcolm could walk (let's face it, *scurry*) around the building until he found the drainpipe and the ivy and Room 11's window. And then, maybe once he was inside, he could find Snip.

CHAPTER 23
AMBERGRIS. ANATOMY. APOLOGIZE.

Malcolm dashed around the building as fast as his mouse-sized legs would take him, clinging to the shadowy bushes and the gravel next to the building. That'd be his ratty instinct kicking in. Hide and cover, it shouted.

That's how, as he dashed behind the dumpster, he ran—nose to nose, whisker to whisker—into another critter. Malcolm squeaked and stopped so suddenly that his back end almost flipped over his front.

"Malcolm?" Clyde was coming out of a hole in the bricks. "Malcolm!"

Malcolm let out a huge breath. "Clyde! What're you doing here?" At the same time, Malcolm realized that he'd been hoping to run into Clyde. Let's face it, Malcolm didn't have a whole lot of friendly, familiar faces left.

"It's my nest," said Clyde. "Come on, I'll show you."
He turned around and started back into the hole. "I just
picked up the best glim. Wait'll you see it. I knew you'd
come back."

Malcolm hung back. "I can't, Clyde, I—"

Clyde stopped and turned slowly. His voice grew hard.
"Deep-fried corn niblets. You're not going to say you need
to go back in again, are you?" He walked around Malcolm,
taking in his tattered ear, his red-sore tail, his scratched
nose, the lumps on the back of his head. "Malcolm, I have
to tell you, this isn't healthy."

Malcolm picked up his tail and tried to smooth it a little.

"I have to." He lifted his head. "Clyde, I'm the only one. There's this cat. She's going to . . . to do *something*."

Clyde snorted. "Pardon me for asking, but how is that any of your business?"

"Well, Aggy needs me. The Academy thinks it's me."

"So what? Malcolm, Snip's fermented right through. Have you seen that collar? I think it's cut off all the air to her brain.

Malcolm put his tail down. "You've met Snip?"

"Well, I've seen her prowling about. You don't live long out here if you aren't aware of all the pouncers." Clyde reached his paw around Malcolm's shoulders. "I like you, Malcolm. And I tell you, going back is going to be nothing but heartache and disappointment. Stay out here! You'll be a fat, happy rat. Sure, it gets a little cold in winter, but we can teach you how to make a nest. Come see mine—it's all dazzly."

Malcolm took a deep breath. "I can't. I have to help the nutters. To find Aggy. To clear my name. To show them not all rats are bad." He glanced at Clyde. "Sorry. I don't mean you, of course. But don't you ever get tired of what everyone thinks of rats?" That last bit burst out of Malcolm like he had been holding his breath. "I mean, we're not all sneaky, dirty, lying, stealing—we're not all skuzzy!"

Clyde leveled his black eyes at Malcolm. They glittered like glim in the moonlight. "Aren't we? Aren't *you*? Look at you, you're skiving around a school at night. That's sneaking. And I hate to break it to you, but you're standing next to garbage right now. Dirty, on top of stealing. And you've already admitted lying is what got you into this mess in the first place. We're *rats*. That's what we do. There's a reason everyone thinks that of us."

Malcolm sighed. There was so much more he wanted to explain. Somehow, he wasn't getting it across. The feeling of confiding in someone like Amelia. The sense of belonging he felt in the classroom as he cuddled with the fifth-graders. The purpose and pride he'd had in joining the Academy.

Couldn't he be a rat *and* have that?

Malcolm took a step backwards. "I've—I've got to go." He squinted. Was that the sun coming up? Gristle, what time was it? He wasn't going to be able to do anything in the day. He needed to get inside before the lankies started arriving or else he'd be stuck outside. No, he'd have to climb the ivy near Room 11 again, then find some place safe to hide out for the day and figure out how exactly to stop Snip and Honey Bunny.

Then tomorrow night, he'd go back to the Fourth. Because there was one place he hadn't been yet. A place that Snip kept mentioning. *"The tall creatures will go up to set the clock. And when they leave the building, you make the call."*

Whatever it was that Snip was up to, Malcolm needed to check the clock tower.

As Malcolm slipped through the window of Room 11, he was amazed that it looked exactly the same. The dry-erase board still listed the fifth-graders who would run the stations for the Dedication Day carnival. Skylar had forgotten to put his chair up—again. Wads of gum clung to the bottom of Kiera's desk.[57] And a polished Granny Smith apple sat in the center of yours, Mr. Binney. Malcolm felt so totally different inside, it seemed like the room should be different, too.

Then Malcolm spied it. And he had to sit down for a moment. There, on the floor, underneath his and Amelia's table, was a hair elastic. Green. Malcolm pictured the green socks Amelia had worn to school. Was that really less than a day ago?

As you know, Mr. Binney, leaving something behind, even something as small as a hair elastic, wasn't something Amelia would do. Malcolm blew out a long breath. What was Amelia thinking? Was she mad? Did she think he bit her on purpose?

When he'd collected himself, Malcolm picked up the hair elastic. It still smelled like strawberry shampoo. But Malcolm steeled himself and crawled up Amelia's chair. He set it gently down at her place on the table. He tried to ignore his super-deluxe cage and Comf-E-Cube. After biting Amelia—even if he could make her understand—he couldn't imagine ever being able to return to them.

---

[57] Malcolm carefully avoided those.

The dictionary sat open on the table. Malcolm rifled through it a little bit. Maybe it was his Knack acting up, but the words *were* lovely. *Ambergris. Anatomy. Apologize.*

Malcolm's tail quivered. Hold on a whisker. He could tell Amelia with this book! He could tell her and furthermore, he could—his tiny heart soared—he could see her again.

Malcolm lifted the page. With his ratty front teeth, he nibbled. He nibbled up and around, until "apologize" drifted free from page 78 of the dictionary. Then he did the same with six other words.[58] And when he was done, he used the antibacterial water to paste them to the table. He stood back.

A—
Apologize · Please still friends
Lamborghini tomorrow
Important —M

---

[58] Let's not tell the librarian about this either. I'm not sure she'd understand.

Would Amelia see? Would she forgive? Would she understand? Would she come?

Only then did Malcolm slip under the classroom door and down the hall to the library. Already the day custodian was unlocking the classrooms and teachers were greeting one another in the lounge. But there was one thing more Malcolm had to check. Another idea itching in the back of his mind. He made a quick detour to the bulletin board outside the library and stood in the hall, staring up at it.

"MCKENNA'S DEDICATION DAY CARNIVAL! Celebrate the 90th Anniversary of McKenna's historic clock tower. Food! Games! Halloween costumes optional. 1–3 p.m., October 29."

Snip had said she was ready for the "big day." Malcolm hadn't heard of any other big days[59] coming up, except this one. And if there was any day that the lankies would turn on the clock, wouldn't it be one in celebration of that clock?

October 29. Malcolm pictured the calendar in Room 11. That was Friday! And today was Thursday, so that meant . . . the lankies would be setting the clock later that night. Whatever Snip was planning, she was doing it *tonight*.

The hall lights flickered. Lankies—Sour Grapes!

Malcolm raced into the library. There was only time for a quick nod toward Oscar. He scurried to the far back cor-

---

[59] Well, he had heard about Winter Break and Snow Days, but from the tone of the nutters discussing them, he suspected they were only the stuff of legends.

ner where he and Amelia had talked last time. Yes, there, on top of the shelf above the car section, the model skeleton rested. And judging from the layer of dust on it, it wasn't used much.

It was a perfect Niche.

Malcolm hesitated, his claws extended. But, yes. He felt certain that it was the right thing to do. The right thing for the rat he was.

Malcolm dragged his claws through the hard plastic of the skull.

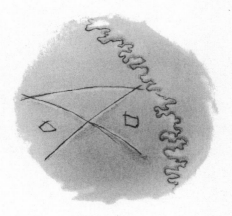

After Marking it, he nestled deep in its cranium. This was his home now.

And he waited for Amelia to show up.

CHAPTER 24
TWIN ENGINES

"Malcolm, are you there? I saw your note."

Malcolm sat up with a start, banging his head on the front of the skull.[60] Where was he? He peeped out of the eye socket. And yanked his head back in so fast that he almost knocked the skeleton over.

Oh, gristle! Oh, scrap!

Malcolm raced around inside his Niche. Oh, *gristle!* What to do?

"It's okay, Malcolm." Malcolm felt the skeleton tip to the side. "Really." An eye peered in at Malcolm.

Only this eye was not Amelia's black-brown one.

It was Jovahn's hazel one.

---

[60] Probably the frontal bone.

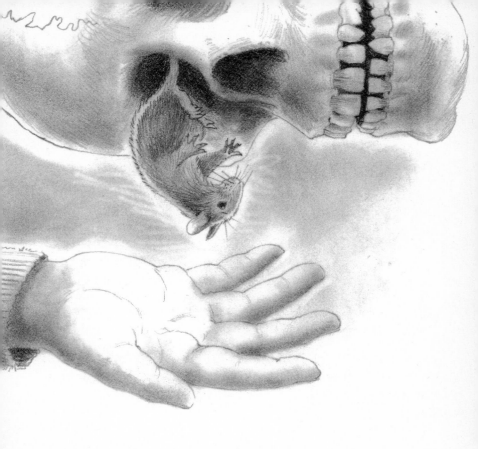

Oh, *scrap*. How had Malcolm already fouled up his first attempt at a Niche? Not to mention ten gazillion other things that were now complicated by the fact that Jovahn was here and not Amelia. Malcolm's head spun as he thought about them all. He knew he was acting like a pup,[61] but he couldn't help it: Malcolm pulled his ears over his eyes and hoped Jovahn would eventually go away.

"Come on, it's not that bad." Jovahn shook the skull a little and Malcolm came tumbling out into his hand.

---

[61] Didn't know that baby rats are called "pups," did you? (Me neither.) But that's just in our country. In Europe they are "kittens." Isn't that weird?

Jovahn held out a peanut butter Ritz cracker. Oh nubbins, that smelled good. Malcolm cracked an eye open.

Jovahn grinned. "See? Now, why don't you tell me why you bit Amelia yesterday?"

Malcolm looked left, then right. Across the library, a class was working on the computers. Where was Amelia? Had she not seen the note at all? Was she mad? Was she absent?

Malcolm wiggled, trying to decide, trying to encourage another nibble offer. Jovahn looked so hopeful. And really, he did already know about Malcolm.

Malcolm hopped from Jovahn's hand to the shelf and an open book. Slowly, he extended a paw. How to put this? "*Shiny. One. Too. Loud.*" Unfortunately, they were still in the car section of books. This one was called *Automotive Heaven.*

Jovahn's eyebrows scrunched together and then cleared. "Shiny one?"

Malcolm pointed to the letter *K* and looked back up.

"Oh! Kiera. You bit Amelia because of Kiera? Oh, she was about to . . ." he said, remembering. "It was *my* fault."

Malcolm bowed his head.

"What do you think you are doing?" A voice pierced the silence.

Both Jovahn and Malcolm squeaked. Jovahn snatched up Malcolm and shoved him behind his back. "Amelia!"

Amelia didn't say another word, just marched forward, her hand held out in front of her. Jovahn started to pull

190

Malcolm out, but then he hesitated. "No. He's not your mouse, Amelia. I want to know him, too."

Amelia glowered like Malcolm had never seen before. Her eyes narrowed. Her fists clenched. Even her silky black ponytail seemed to crackle with energy. "You—you," she sputtered. Finally, she set her shoulders. "You don't need him."

"What?" Jovahn was so surprised that Malcolm thought for a second that he was going to drop him.

Amelia looked away. "You heard me. You've got a million friends. Everyone in class is probably counting the minutes until you come back."

"What?" Jovahn said again. "Like they aren't waiting for you?"

Amelia pulled the end of her ponytail. Malcolm saw that she was wearing her green hair elastic. But her socks were white with orange pumpkins. What did that mean?

"They aren't," she spit out. "Not in the same way. They like to be around you."

"Well, they like to be around you, too. Geez, we wouldn't be able to do our morning schedule without you to correct it for Mr. Binney. And, look at Dedication Day. We'd be without anything to drink if you hadn't pointed it out to the PTA."

An exasperated sigh rushed out of Amelia. She finally raised her eyes to Jovahn's. "No one cares about that stuff. Not *really*. You know what I mean. No one's missing *me*." She swallowed. "Except maybe Malcolm."

191

Jovahn stared at Amelia for a second. He opened his mouth like he was about to say something. He scuffed his untied basketball shoe.

Then he held out Malcolm.

Malcolm jumped into Amelia's hand. Oh, it was good to be back with her. He didn't know it was possible, but something close to a purr bubbled out of him.

Jovahn said quietly, "If you really want to know, no one cares about me acting like a numb-brain either. Not really. They only like something to laugh about and I give it to them."

They stood there, eyeing each other while the class across the library clacked on their computer keys. Jovahn and Amelia seemed to be deciding something. It reminded Malcolm of the rarest kinds of customers at the Pet Emporium. Some customers snatched up whichever pet was closest. Most based their decision on the cuteness factor. But there were some—not many—who waited. They studied the critters first. They watched, they observed. Then they picked their pet.

Finally, Amelia flipped her ponytail over her shoulder and said, "Maybe we should let Malcolm decide." She set Malcolm back down on *Automotive Heaven*.

Malcolm shrank as small as a mouse at first. What? Him? Why? He could never not choose Amelia. But leave out Jovahn? Malcolm didn't want to hurt him either. He seemed like a good nutter. And he did have tasty snacks.

Then Malcolm realized that there was another choice. A choice that was right for him. Because if it came right down to it, he'd miss them both. It was part of the reason why he was trying to get back to Room 11, wasn't it?

Malcolm scanned the page. He pointed. Amelia and Jovahn drew their heads together. "*Twin. Engines.*"

Amelia understood first. Maybe she was better at deciphering Malcolm because she'd done it longer. Or maybe she wasn't distracted by the photo of the black Porsche above Malcolm's words like Jovahn was. But whatever the reason, she knew.

"Really?" she whispered. "Are you sure?"

Malcolm pulled at his whiskers and nodded. Amelia took a deep breath.

"What? What?" Jovahn said. "Oh! I get it. He wants both of us, doesn't he?"

Amelia nodded slowly.

A grin as wide as a basketball court spread on Jovahn's face. "Well, that's good, right? I mean, who says you can only have one friend in the world? Then you start acting as snooty and as snotty as Tianna and Kiera. Two is better than one, right?"

Maybe Jovahn wasn't such a numb-brain neanderthal after all.

"Maybe," Amelia said. "Well, Malcolm, if you're sure . . ." Amelia glanced over her shoulder at the clock and class working. "We're running out of time. Hang on."

She darted across the library and came back with a dictionary. "What's happened?"

Malcolm sniffed the volume. Oooh—a collegiate version!

Then Malcolm told them about what he had heard in the basement the night before. About Snip working with someone. About how the nutters were in danger. About how he must find Aggy. Tonight.

Jovahn interrupted only once. "Wait—you used whose phone?" A incredulous grin spread across his face.

"Oh, shut up," said Amelia, elbowing him. "You're missing the point. Go on, Malcolm."

Malcolm continued, finishing with, "*Must. Go. Tonight.*" He waited for Amelia to argue like last time.

But she was quiet. It was Jovahn who spoke. "Wow, you're the man, Malcolm. I mean, you know, the mouse. I wish we could go with you."

Malcolm stopped and looked up at Amelia. She cleared her throat. "Actually, Malcolm's a rat."

"What?"

Amelia nodded. So did Malcolm. Jovahn laughed. "Well, then, Malcolm, you're the *rat*."

Amelia frowned. "But why would Snip *tell* Malcolm to go to the clock tower? It doesn't make sense."

Both Jovahn and Malcolm shrugged. Jovahn added, "How can he not go? Even if Aggy's not there, Malcolm might find something else out. Something that Snip didn't expect him to."

194

"Yeah, the ghost of McKenna," Amelia muttered. "I don't like it."

Malcolm paged through the dictionary. "*Rat. Be. Careful.*"

Amelia looked doubtful. "That's supposed to make us feel better?" She sighed. "How are we supposed to know if you're in trouble?"

Jovahn's smile faded. "What if we meet back here tomorrow morning at nine? If you're not here, we'll know something happened. We'll—we'll come get you. Or something. If Amelia can steal a phone—"

"I didn't steal it, I—"

"—if Amelia can 'borrow' a phone without the owner's permission"—Jovahn dodged Amelia's kick—"I can pull the fire alarm. Or something. Clear the school so we can go up and get you."

Malcolm's whiskers twitched. How could Honey Bunny ever think knowing nutters like this was a bad thing?

Across the library, the class started gathering their stuff. Amelia said, "Come on, we'd better put Malcolm back. Where'd you find him?"

Jovahn tipped the model skeleton and plunked Malcolm back into the skull. "Same time tomorrow, Malcolm?"

Malcolm nodded. Amelia hesitated, then stuck a finger in an eye socket and scratched Malcolm between the ears. "Be safe, okay?" It was the same hand Malcolm had bitten. She smiled sadly as he nuzzled the Band-Aid wrapped around her thumb. "I know. You had to. It's okay, Malcolm."

Jovahn had taken a few steps toward the door, then came back. But he wasn't looking at Malcolm.

Amelia pulled at the sleeve of his soccer jersey. "We'd better go."

His hand reached out. "Just a minute. I think—well, I think I'm gonna check out this *Automotive Heaven*. It looks pretty cool." He glanced up at the model skeleton with a grin. "You don't mind, do you, Malcolm?"

CHAPTER 25

THE CLOCK TOWER

As midnight approached, Malcolm felt like he had a whole box of paper clips in his stomach.

Finally, the building settled and Malcolm could steal out of the library. He detoured by the aquarium after an insistent splash. He read, "HEARD THE PLAN. BE CRITTER-WISE."

Malcolm nodded. "Thanks, Oscar."

And then it was off to locker 2135 and up to the fourth floor.

It didn't take Malcolm long before he realized he had no idea how to get up to the clock tower. It's not like there was a sign with a big arrow. Malcolm crept from shadow to shadow, focusing on the heavy, locked doors without windows. The doors most people walk by without seeing: utility closets, supply rooms, and storage areas of a school—you know, the boiler rooms.

Malcolm was scooting out from yet another bathroom door when he heard voices. Human voices. Yes, that's right, Mr. Binney. *Your* voice. And Ms. Brumble's.

Coming from *above* Malcolm.

Malcolm followed the sounds of your discussion. It's not like you were trying to be quiet about it. You probably assumed that you were alone up there. I mean, who would think that a rat who was your escaped mouse was listening in? At midnight?

Your voices were how Malcolm found the old wooden door. It must have been covered by junk before, because Malcolm could see where you had pulled the heavy desks and stacks of chairs aside. They left huge swaths of dust scraped off the floor.

"Come on, Ronnie, you've set the clock, let's get back downstairs. Remember what happened last time we were up here?"

"Shhh, Mark. That's just it. I was thinking about the times we've been up here in the past year."

"What on earth are you talking about? You know, tomorrow's a busy day, we've got the carnival, I'm going to need all the sleep I can get—"

"Just sit, Mr. Binney! There's something I need to know. I don't want to wait any longer."

Malcolm snuck under the door, and he heard the tone in Ms. Brumble's voice drop lower. "First of all, I'm sorry

198

about your class's mouse, Mark. I know it's hard to lose a pet. But chasing your mouse yesterday reminded me all over again—we're a good team. And do you remember when we came up here last August? When you helped me board up those windows and you smashed your thumb with the hammer? That was when I knew, Knew with a capital *K*. And I've been thinking about it all these months since."

You were right, Mr. Binney. What on earth was she babbling about? Malcolm had never heard Ms. Brumble's voice so full of, of . . . wobbliness.

Malcolm crept through a stack of paint cans and finally saw you and the room.

This room—the bottom of the clock tower—couldn't have been any older than the rest of the school, but it sure looked like it was. The ancient wood floor was scuffed to a dusty gray color. Plaster crumbled off the walls in chunks so that the boards underneath shone through like ugly scabs. And every flat surface was scrawled with words. Some faded, some bold. Malcolm felt his Knack prickle to attention. *Tony—Class of 1952. McKenna Knights Rule. Sophie '88. Mark* ♥ *Veronica.* Pen, pencil, marker, paint— the words covered everything as far as a ratty eye could see.[62]

You sat on a sagging staircase that stretched up the far outside wall, Mr. Binney. Ms. Brumble stood on the floor below. Her eyebrow hoop flashed in the moonlight that streamed in through the white clock face high above. Her shoulders shook a little. Then she lowered a knee to the dusty floor and cleared her throat. "Mark Binney, will you marry me?"

Malcolm saw your mouth fall open into a perfect *O.* "What?"

"I have to say it again?"

You ran your hands through your hair. "No . . ." You started fumbling in your shirt pocket.

"Oh! Well—" She flushed and started to rise.

"No!" You grabbed her hand and pulled her down next

---

[62] Which, to be sure, isn't really all that far, since rats rely more on their senses of smell and hearing and touch. But still. Lots of graffiti. I'm a little surprised Ms. Brumble could stand it.

to you. "I mean yes. Yes, Veronica Brumble, I will marry you."

You finally pulled something out of your pocket. Malcolm leaned forward. It was the blue velvet box! For the Grumble of the Brumble? Sweet nubbins. And hold on a whisker. Suddenly Malcolm felt more than a little confuddled, and there was no brew within sniffing distance. The words on the wall: *Mark* ♥ *Veronica*. The Grumble of the Brumble? Ronnie Brumble = *Veronica* Brumble?

"I was going to ask you!" you said. "I have a ring. *Had* a ring. For weeks I've been carrying it around. It's—you're not going to believe this—"

But all the excitement had stirred up the dust. Malcolm's nose wrinkled. His whiskers shuddered.

"Ah—ah—ah—choo!"

Now, a rat sneeze isn't much. Especially one from a rat the size of Malcolm. It certainly wasn't enough to turn your head, Mr. Binney. It was pressed too tightly against Ms. Brumble's.

But there are other creatures who listen for the sneezes of rats. Their whole beings are tuned to the slightest, smallest hint that dinner—*prey*—might be available. And I'm not talking about cats.

It was that itty-bitty sneeze that caused a white, flapping object to swoop down with a shriek. And all three of you—Malcolm, you, and Ms. Brumble—echoed that screech in your own voices.

"The ghost of McKenna!"

The ghost spun down. It was everywhere, battering the steps, the air, the curving banister. All the while, screaming.

You ducked, Mr. Binney. But it flapped right past you. You grabbed Ms. Brumble's hand and pulled her out to the safety of the hall.

The ghost didn't chase you. No, it had its huge yellow eyes on one thing. Something it had been waiting for for months. Something it had been hungering for for ages.

Malcolm.

Well, maybe not Malcolm *specifically*. But Malcolm would do. The ghost banked and dove. Wide white limbs stretched out in deadly silence. As the ghost descended on him, Malcolm knew two things. First, terror like he had never experienced. He had never been hunted before, but something deep inside him Knew that his moments left alive in this world were less than he could count on his claws.

And second, Malcolm knew that *this* was the reason Snip had sent him here. There was no Aggy. There was only a sure death by means of the ghost of McKenna. And Snip had known it and had planned for it to happen all along.

With an inaudible flap, the ghost swooped at Malcolm, barely stirring the dust on the floor. Malcolm only had time to gasp "Aggy!" before talons reached out and lifted him. And with a stomach-dropping lurch, Malcolm was airborne. Flying up.

Past the rickety stairs.

To the top of the clock tower.

CHAPTER 26
THE GHOST OF McKENNA

The ghost let out another cry as it landed on the edge of a tall, clear plastic box in the center of the top of the clock tower floor. Inside it, the mechanism for the clock clicked and rasped. Hanging upside down, Malcolm spied piles of feathers, bird droppings, and bits and pieces of small creatures on the dusty floor.

Then the ghost tossed Malcolm to its curved beak.

Have you guessed what the ghost of McKenna is yet, Mr. Binney? Malcolm didn't really have a name for it, but he knew it wasn't a supernatural ghostly being. (Those talons pinched a little too hard for that.) No, he was caught and about to be eaten by what is known by lankies and nutters as a barn owl.

Malcolm found himself headfirst inside the owl's mouth. He didn't have time to think. Which was maybe a good thing, because before the beak pressed down to squish and swallow him, Malcolm yelped.

"Wait! Please!"

The outburst was enough to cause the owl to pause. The owl was not used to having his food talk back, maybe. He didn't let go, but he didn't bite down, either. The owl just stopped for a moment, surprised.

It was warm and sticky inside the owl's mouth, and it didn't smell so good, either. Malcolm knew he had to talk fast. "Um, wait. Please. Don't eat me. Perhaps—" Malcolm thought quickly. It had worked with Snip, even though Snip had been the one to lure him into this situation. "Maybe I can help you?"

Silence. Then a low rumble came up from the owl's throat. The owl shook. Gusts of air pushed on Malcolm. Finally, the owl's beak opened and Malcolm wiggled free. The owl, with its mouth empty now, erupted in hoots.

Malcolm scampered to the far side of the plastic clock-work box. It backed against a wall and Malcolm clambered up it to the safety of a low rafter. Graffiti scarred the worn surface of this, too.

Meanwhile, the owl hooted in laughter.

"You? Help me?" the owl said finally, in a voice that was as deep and dark as the night without a moon. The owl poked a wing up at Malcolm. Malcolm felt the whisper-soft edge of the feathers brush him. "You can come on out. I won't eat you."

Malcolm peered around the rafter. Somehow he got the sense that this critter wasn't like Snip—that if he said it was safe, he'd keep his word. Malcolm leaned over the edge of the rafter beam.

That's when he came face to face with the grandeur of a barn owl. The wide white circular disks around the yellow eyes. The snowy pelt. That voice! No wonder people thought he was a ghost.

The owl studied Malcolm. "Not much to you, is there? No more than a taste. I'm Beert, by the way. Congratulations on not being eaten. But I'm almost as bored as I am hungry up here. That was delightful. So, what did you have in mind?"

"H—how long have you been up here?" Malcolm glanced around. Filtered moonlight shone through the cloudy glass of the clock faces, but the rest of the tower was dark in shadows.

Beert sighed. "Since last summer. Excuse me, what did you say your name was?"

"Um, I'm Malcolm. So why don't you go out?"

"Out? I'd love to. But the windows, you see." Beert gestured with a wing. Malcolm could see that the tower had once had arched windows on either side of the clock faces. But they had been boarded over.

Malcolm frowned and climbed down. He hopped over

to one of the windows. "But can't you—why don't you—" Malcolm clawed at a corner of the wood. It crumbled away. "It's not strong."

Beert brushed a wing against it. A long white speckled feather floated free. "To you, maybe. I can't. This beak and these talons are for hunting, not scratching."

"Oh. Yeah," Malcolm said, rubbing his neck where Beert had grabbed him. He had gotten so used to being able to go where he wanted. Beert was as caged as a critter at the Pet Emporium. Slowly, an idea formed in Malcolm's head. "Do you want out?"

"Oh, starlit skies, *yes*. I call to Hestia every night." Beert's deep voice rose into a screech.

Malcolm winced. "I know. We can hear you below."

The owl regarded him. "Really? Then why in heavens would you come up here?"

"Well, I didn't know you were an owl, for one thing. I thought you were a ghost."

Beert blinked. "And so I ask again. Why in heavens would you come up here?"

"It's a long story. A really long story." Malcolm turned back to the wood and tried a bite with his teeth. Yes! Look at how quickly he could gnaw right through this! He could help Beert and then . . . and then . . . what exactly *was* Malcolm going to do next? The clock tower was supposed to hold the answers. But there was no Aggy here. There was nothing but a tormented owl.

The owl in question folded his wings behind him. "I'm listening," he said. "I've been up here for so very long all by myself."

Malcolm told him everything. And that's how Malcolm and Beert formed the first owl-rat friendship in the history of the animal kingdom. Oh, I know, you hear about animals like these bonding all the time in children's books. But it doesn't really happen like that in the wild. Or even in the wilds of an old school, for that matter. In nature, a friendship like this is usually permanently damaged by one friend eating the other.

But Beert was as good as his word. And while they talked, Malcolm clawed at the edge of the particle board. It was comforting, kind of like chewing his whiskers. Soon, the moon shone bright through a hole the size of Jovahn's fist.

Beert walked forward, awkward on his long talons. He leaned down and poked his beak through the opening. He flapped his wings a little and gave his tail a wiggle. He let out a shrill call. An answering one came back within seconds. Malcolm shivered.

"Oh! I can hear my Hestia in the oaks." Beert pulled his head out. He blinked his huge eyes rapidly. Malcolm began to gnaw again as Beert fluttered around the tower. "You said Snip is planning this for Dedication Day? But what is that?"

Malcolm stopped gnawing. "A carnival in the courtyard. A party." He remembered the poster. "Honoring the clock tower. There's snacks, and nutters wear their Halloween cos—"

"Halloween?" said Beert. "Oh, Hestia and I used to have such fun scaring the sugar out of kids on Halloween. It's amazing what a good Swoop and Call can do. My record is four pants wettings in one night!" He preened his feathers. "But—did you say this clock?"

Malcolm nodded. "She said when the lankies set the clock and leave the tower."

Beert dropped his wing down and spluttered, "But they've set the clock. Can't you hear it running? Why in moonlight are you still here? Whatever this Snip is doing, she's doing it tonight. Right now!"

Malcolm gulped and groaned. "I know! But I don't know what else to do. I'm finally here in the clock tower. And there's only you—no offense."

"But surely there's something! You must do something."

"Like what?"

Beert was quiet. Malcolm busied himself at the board again. See, even the owl couldn't think of anything. Malcolm had failed.

Finally, the great owl swiveled his head around to face Malcolm behind him. "Malcolm, that cat—Snip—is pure, warped, twisted evil. She may have started out as someone's pet at one time, but whatever has happened to her in the years since has twisted and changed her inside so all she wants is to hurt. Maybe it's revenge. Maybe it's for fun by now. But she's got to be stopped. She's the reason I'm here." He turned his head back to the wall so Malcolm couldn't see his face. His voice was soft. "I picked this place for our nest. Hestia wasn't so sure. But I thought it was the perfect place for our eggs and later, our owlets—safe, out of the wind and rain." He nodded to a pile of sticks that

Malcolm hadn't noticed before. "It was right over there in the corner. Then one night, Hestia was hunting, and I left them for just a second. Snip stole up here and ate our owlets. They didn't even have feathers yet." His voice shook.

"As if that wasn't enough, she took my Hestia away from me, too. I was intent, I'll admit, on hunting Snip. Such a scrawny cat! I could catch her easily, I thought. And she deserved to die. But one night while my Hestia was out, that cat lured me down to the fourth floor. It was that tail tip. I couldn't take my eyes off it. I chased her through halls and rooms. Well, she must have heard the people's plan, because when I came back up to our roost, I was closed in. The windows boarded up. And my Hestia sealed out."

Beert's voice turned to a growl. "I've lost everything because of that cat. She needs to be stopped before she hurts more critters."

Malcolm didn't know what to say. He remembered that weaving white-tipped tail of Snip's. How it had been so hard, so hard to look away. Had Aggy been drawn to it, too?

"Beert, I'm so sorry."

"There's more. Maybe this is nothing, but maybe it's not," Beert continued. "There is something else on the fourth floor. I hear it at night,[63] rattling deep in the pipes.

---

[63] According to Amelia's encyclopedia, owls have a remarkable sense of hearing.

The radiators, maybe. Do you know the old science room? The one across from the elevator? It comes from there, but only when the cat is gone."

Malcolm spit out a mouthful of wood. After all this time, finally a sign of Aggy? "I do," he whispered. "I do know that room. Here," he said, stepping back, "can you fit through?"

Beert pumped his wings. His voice quivered with excitement. "Yes. Yes, I think so!"

A shriek from the oak trees outside echoed in the tower. Beert twitched, then ducked and started wiggling through the hole. He twisted his head around one more time. "Malcolm. Thank you. You're a fine rat. I know you'll do the right thing. I'm proud to not have eaten you."

And with that, Beert pushed off and soared out into the air. Malcolm caught a glimpse of a white shadow swoop by and heard a screech that would wet the pants of any kindergartner —if one were still awake.

CHAPTER 27
MIDNIGHT

Malcolm had taken not more than two steps when a gruff voice called out, "You're not going anywhere." A white mass of fur, silky soft and as plush as a stuffed animal, hopped to the top of the stairs.

Malcolm whirled around. "Honey Bunny!"

Honey Bunny here, now? It was true then.

Honey Bunny scowled and hopped closer. "Don't call me that."

Malcolm could smell the banana chips on him. Honey Bunny reached out and poked Malcolm with a clawed paw. "I've been following you, rat."

Malcolm winced. He didn't have time to mess with Honey Bunny right now. He needed to get downstairs!

But unless you could fly like Beert, the only way out of the tower was past the rabbit.

Honey Bunny jabbed again, and Malcolm stumbled backwards over his own tail. "You think you've got everyone fooled, don't you, rat? Aggy, those nitwit hamsters, even, somehow, the owl who just left. But I know. I know. Polly and Tank saw rat tracks up on the Fourth. So tonight, I followed *you*. You've been looking all over the Fourth tonight for your pal the cat, haven't you?" He reached out and twanged Malcolm's growing-out whiskers.

Have you ever noticed that sometimes it's the littlest thing that can trigger something huge?

Well, that touch. That twang. Honey Bunny's pinky claw set off an eruption inside Malcolm. It was like pouring Mentos into a bottle of soda. Everything churned and bubbled up: Getting kicked out of the Academy. Being mistaken for a mouse. Being distrusted for his rattiness. And it was all because of Honey Bunny! Honey Bunny and his blustering, narrow-thinking ways.

It all came gushing out.

"*You* know?" Malcolm exploded, taking a step forward. Honey Bunny blinked and his ears drew back. "You *know*? *I* know. I know what you've been up to behind everyone else's back. How you hate being a pet. All those sticky fingers and pink ribbons! And the Academy's not much better, is it? Aggy—so trusting, so slow. Now, with Aggy out of the way, you can be in charge—"

POW! Malcolm flew backwards as what felt like a fluff-covered bowling ball hit him. The two critters somersaulted across the floor of the clock tower. "How—*dare*—you!" Honey Bunny huffed as he tried to pin Malcolm down.

Malcolm dodged and managed to plant a kick on Honey Bunny's side. It didn't move the massive rabbit, but it shifted his weight enough that Malcolm could wiggle out from under him.

But Honey Bunny wasn't letting Malcolm off that easily. Honey Bunny lunged again. Malcolm took a step backwards, toward the glass clock face. He was running out of room. He looked frantically around. Where to go? Behind him, the moon glowed through the cloudy white glass. Metal rods and supports connected the clock to the gear box in the center of the tower.

Malcolm leaped onto a rod and crept along it to one of the metal bands on the face of the clock.

Below him, from the dusty wood floor, Honey Bunny tried to follow. But his long rear paws weren't meant for climbing. Let's face it, rabbits don't have the dexterity[64] that rats do.[65] He slipped and fell off the rod. He growled. Malcolm didn't even know it was possible for bunnies to growl, but he did. He swiped at Malcolm with a paw full of sharp claws.

Malcolm was out of reach.

---

[64] Dexterity = ability to grasp something. Not a vocabulary word, but sometimes there's only one right word.

[65] And let's face it: that tail of his—cute, yes. But utterly useless.

"I *saw* you," the rabbit fumed, pacing. "I've been following Snip for ages. And last night I tracked her down the elevator to the basement. She met with a critter in the boiler room. She's been waiting for the right critter for a long time. I saw her leave. Then I saw YOU come out after her, so tonight I followed you." He hopped back and forth on the floor.

"What?" Malcolm fumed. "You saw me yesterday because you were meeting with her. I heard you."

Outside, the hands of the clock clicked a minute over. He had to think to get out of here. The metal supports were narrow—a paw's width, at most. Good thing he wasn't a large rat. Malcolm pulled himself up higher. If he could sneak across the clock, he could maybe make a jump for the banister to the staircase. And from there, he might be able to lose Honey Bunny in all the junk on the fourth floor.

Malcolm clambered up to the X.[66]

Honey Bunny tried a new tactic. He walked up the braces on the side of the clockwork box and hopped on top of it. The two critters were now eye to eye but several feet apart in the tower. He snarled, "I was in the hall." He drew himself up. He really was a colossal rabbit. "And I saw—YOU!"

With his final word, Honey Bunny sprang. His powerful back legs stretched as he launched himself straight at Malcolm.

---

[66] It should be obvious by now that Malcolm is a quick learner, but he hadn't yet heard about roman numerals.

Malcolm felt the glass crunch behind him. For a moment, it held the weight of the two critters against it. Then the cold of the night air was at Malcolm's back as the glass fell away in chunks.

Malcolm reached out to grab anything he could. He hooked his hind toes and tail into a number below. Honey Bunny clawed for a grasp, too. He clung on the bottom edge of the clock face, his extra-long back feet barely on it. The courtyard, far below, was a vast inky void.

Malcolm pressed himself flat against the clock face. He gasped for breath. From above, Malcolm saw Honey

Bunny was cut, a slash on a silky ear. It dripped dark blood down Honey Bunny's back. Malcolm shook his head. Honey Bunny was so *certain* that Malcolm was with Snip.

The rabbit's words echoed in Malcolm's head. He was in the hall? Malcolm remembered the *thump* that had halted Snip's conversation. But if the rabbit was in the hall . . . Malcolm shook his head again. He needed to think this through.

But there was no time. Honey Bunny was moving. He reached up for Malcolm, his pink eyes narrowed.

"Wait!" Malcolm scrambled to the top of the IX. How to change the mind of a rabbit who was so convinced of Malcolm's rat finkiness that he was willing to risk it all to stop him?

"Honey Bunny," Malcolm shouted. "It's not me! You have to believe me! I *was* in the boiler room last night, but I was hiding, listening. Listening to Snip talk to someone that I thought was you."

"Me?" the rabbit roared, as his foot slipped.

From inside the clock tower came a long, low cackle. A white tail tip holding a long

219

owl feather weaved back and forth through the hold in the clock face.

"Snip!" Malcolm whispered under his breath—at the exact same time as Honey Bunny did. Honey Bunny jerked his head toward Malcolm.

Had she been there the whole time?

Snip let go of the feather, and it drifted in the darkness. She pulled her tail in and stuck her head through the hole. "Don't let me interrupt you two," she said. "This is priceless. Please, go on."

The clock clicked a minute forward. Honey Bunny's long foot slipped again. His claws scratched into the bottom edge of the clock as he tried to get a better grip. He glanced down at the blackness of the courtyard below. The feather had disappeared.

Malcolm talked fast, before Snip could twist things. "Honey Bunny, you have to believe me. Snip is using the Academy."

Snip smirked down at Honey Bunny. "Honey Bunny," she purred, drawing his name out. "You're going to miss all the excitement tomorrow. You always are a smidge too slow. Embarrassing, isn't it?"

And now, Malcolm Knew. Knew with a capital *K*. He'd been all wrong about Honey Bunny. There was no way that the two were working together. Because if they were, Honey Bunny would never have allowed Snip to call him by his full name.

"It's not what you think," Malcolm rushed on. "Snip's planning something, tonight. And it's bigger than Aggy."

Snip hissed at Malcolm, "You are a good listener." She stretched her whiskers wide in a sharp grin. "No matter now, though. You're too late." She faked a yawn. "Did you know that it's supposed to be a nice sunny fall day for Dedication Day tomorrow? It'll be hot under those tents with those Halloween costumes on. And all the treats! Candy, popcorn. Yes, I've been watching the carnival for many years now. Those nutters, as you call them, will be awfully thirsty."

Honey Bunny looked from Snip to Malcolm and back to Snip again. Another minute clicked by and his left paw slipped completely off. "What's she talking about, rat?"

Malcolm gulped. "I—I don't really know. She's brought her brew down to the boiler room. It's something to ruin Dedication Day tomorrow."

"The boiler room," Honey Bunny said slowly. "It's—"

Malcolm thought of the pipes and tanks in the boiler room, pumping heat, pumping water. He remembered the smell and how confuddled it made Polly and him. A sick feeling rose in his stomach. "She's going to put her brew in the school's water," Malcolm whispered.

His eyes met Honey Bunny's. Coffee-black and rose-pink.

Two critters on the same side.

A wheezy cackle from Snip. "Have fun, pets," she called, as she pulled her head back inside.

"You really aren't helping her," Honey Bunny said. It wasn't a question.

Malcolm shook his head. There was urgency before, but somehow knowing exactly what Snip was planning made it all worse. They had to get off this clock!

"Listen," Honey Bunny said. The clock clicked again and his right rear paw began to slip. "I'm not going to get off this. You have to—"

"What do you mean?" A new sense of panic rose in Malcolm. He shimmied to the center of the clock and tried to reach down. "Come on, we can climb back through."

"I can't, Malcolm." Even under the fluffy fur, Malcolm could see the muscles straining on the rabbit. He really was remarkably strong.

The minute hand moved again. Both hands, pointing straight up.

Bong!

The entire tower vibrated with the noise. Malcolm's head rattled.

Bong!

"Malcolm!"

Malcolm looked over. Honey Bunny was hanging off the clock with one paw.

"Honey Bunny!" Malcolm reached for him. But he was only the size of a mouse.

The rabbit kicked with his hind legs as his paws slipped even further. "Malcolm—Aggy—the Ripe Tomato—"

Bong!

And then, Honey Bunny fell off.

"Honey Bunny!" Malcolm shrieked as loud as a barn owl.

Bong!

Malcolm turned his face to the clock. Oh, scrap. What had he done?

The last few minutes of conversation ran through Malcolm's head again. But it all sounded different now. His stomach twisted. Nubbins, he was as guilty as Honey Bunny! Honey Bunny had made up his mind about Malcolm and couldn't see anything else . . . and Malcolm had done the exact same thing about Honey Bunny.

Now both of them had missed who was really working with Snip.

Bong!

Bong!

Bong!

The clock seemed to chime on and on. When it finally stopped, all Malcolm could hear was the whistling wind. He uncurled himself. His body was stiff and cold.

Malcolm pulled himself over to look through the broken clock face into the tower. Everything inside was dark and still. He took a deep breath. Even if he had been so wrong about Honey Bunny, Snip still needed to be stopped.

And now, with Honey Bunny . . . gone, it was up to Malcolm.

CHAPTER 28
VALOR AND MERIT

Now, I know what you're thinking, Mr. Binney. About
how Malcolm should have gone to get help, right? Gone
back to Room 11 and left another note. Found an Academy
member and risked telling them everything, maybe.
Crumb, maybe even knocked a phone off a hook and di-
aled 911. But Malcolm didn't. It might be one of the inherent[67] qualities of people (rats) with true merit and valor:
Sometimes they act without thinking things all the way
through. Because if they did, they'd be regular folks. Like
you or me.

So, no. Malcolm didn't go get help. He knew Snip had
to be stopped. And Aggy saved. And he planned to use

---

[67] Inherent = a quality that is in something naturally. Amelia is inherently neat.
Vocabulary from 12/2.

every ratty fiber and trick in his body to do that. Especially now that Honey Bunny was gone.

A critter reveals his true self at midnight, after all.

Malcolm cautiously crept out into the fourth floor hallway again. Far off, his ratty sense of hearing picked up a familiar whirring. Malcolm scurried down the hall and around the corner in time to see the elevator doors shutting.

So Snip had gone downstairs. Well, at least Malcolm knew she wasn't up here and he could move out in the open. That would make his search faster. Because, yes, he was going to take one last look for Aggy. Buzzing in his head were Honey Bunny's last words. Aggy had called a *Ripe Tomato*. Malcolm's mind flashed back to that night in the kindergarten room. Honey Bunny dialing the phone, summoning the Academy with those words. If Aggy could call a Ripe Tomato, she must be okay, right?

Malcolm raced down the center of the hall. It seemed extra dark after the moonlight in the clock tower. He used his growing-out whiskers to guide him.

Which didn't work out so well. Because rounding the corner to the science room, Malcolm ran smack into something in the middle of the hall. Something so big that Malcolm flew tail over nose.

Something large and firm, and . . . scaly.

"Aggy!" Malcolm whispered. Out here in the open? After all this time?

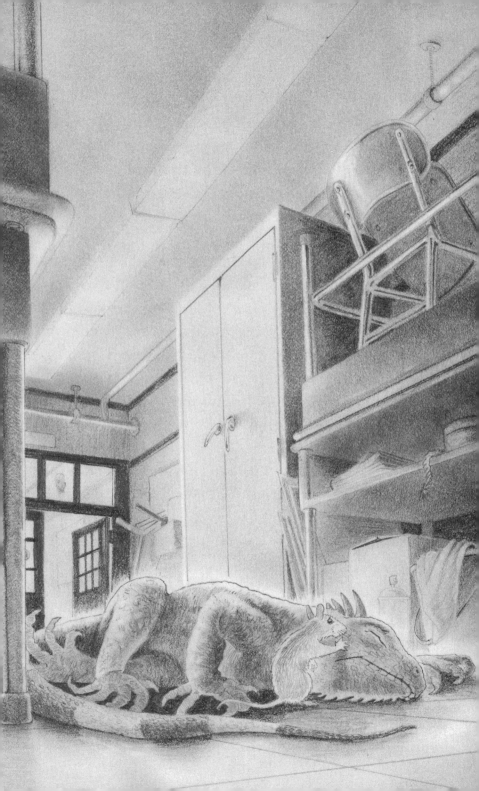

But who cared? Aggy was here! Malcolm had found Aggy!

"Aggy, I can't believe you're here! Do you know all that's happening? Why haven't you come back? Everyone's looking for you! And Snip—Snip is going to do something to the nutters. Tonight! Come on, let's go. Snip is downstairs. We can make it out of here before she comes back!" Malcolm pulled on Aggy's leg. Why wasn't she moving? Why wasn't she answering? "Aggy?" Malcolm whispered.

But there—Malcolm felt, more than saw, Aggy's bulging eyes slowly blink open. "Malcolm," Aggy said. Her voice was raspy and weak. "Blessed greens. You're here."

"Aggy, really, we've got to get you out of here. I can explain when we get back to our floor." Malcolm shot a glance down the hall at the elevator.

Aggy's eyes closed. "I'm not going anywhere, Malcolm."

Malcolm, who had been tugging at Aggy's tail now, paused. "What? We have to go. We don't know when Snip will come back."

"Malcolm. Stop." Aggy's voice had a little more oomph behind it, but it faded fast. "I can't go anywhere. I'm too cold. The radiator was barely warm enough to keep me alive with that broken window in the science room . . ." Her voice trailed off. "It's been too long."

The science room. The radiator! Of course—Aggy was cold-blooded. The only way for her to survive away from her heat lamp this long would be near something warm. It must have been Aggy whom Beert had heard rattling in the radiators.

Malcolm rose up on his hind legs and tugged again. "Well, let's get you back there. You can warm up first—"

Aggy shook her head. More like a slow-motion sway in one direction. "We can't. She broke it."

Malcolm sat back on all fours. "Aggy, Snip has plans for tonight. She wants to distract the Academy so—oh!" He sat down on the floor next to Aggy. "This is it. *You're* it. The distraction. The Ripe Tomato. You didn't call it, but the Academy is on their way, aren't they?"

Aggy creaked out a nod. "The Academy is coming upstairs. And Snip is going down." Her tongue flicked in and out with a faint hissing noise.

"To put her brew in the water in the boiler room!" Malcolm finished. "Aggy, that stuff, her brew, it's foul. But Snip is crazy. She can't really hurt anyone with it, right?"

Aggy managed a weak twitch of a smile. "I always knew you were a smart rat. But it comes down to this: Does it matter if her brew works? Do we want her to try it on the nutters we love?"

She was right. But Malcolm couldn't leave Aggy up here. Where was that Ripe Tomato? He pressed next to her. Maybe the heat from his tiny body could warm her a little. Suddenly, he drew back. "Wait. Did you call me a—"

Aggy slowly curled her tail around Malcolm. "A rat.

Yes, I've always known. As a critter with a magnificent tail myself, it makes it easier to recognize one in other species."

"So you knew I lied?" Malcolm sure didn't feel magnificent right then.

"I guess I didn't think of it as a lie. I thought you weren't ready to tell us yet." Aggy closed her eyes again and seemed to fall asleep.

Crumb, Aggy had known this whole time. And it didn't matter to her. Malcolm rubbed her side. She was so cold!

It seemed important to keep Aggy talking. "But, Aggy, why? Why is Snip doing this?"

She took a ragged breath. "I can only guess, of course. Snip's been up here so long, Malcolm. Alone with only spiders, decaying science supplies, hate, and bitterness to keep her company. It's festered to the point where she wants to hurt anyone who's not as lonely and angry and *stuck* as she is."

"Like the nutters," Malcolm said. *Like Beert*, he thought.

"Or the Midnight Academy," Aggy added. "This—me up here, her brew downstairs—fixes them both in her mind, I guess." Her voice faded and she laid her head down on the cold tile.

Malcolm couldn't let her sleep. He had to keep her awake until someone got here! "What happened that night, Aggy? Why'd you leave your room?"

Aggy stirred, but didn't lift her head or open her eyes.

"I should have known better." She whispered, "It was the tail."

"The tail?" Malcolm thought of that twitching, twisting white tip.

"I heard Snip in the hall. It was dark; even the emergency lights were out. But I could see her tail. And she had something, was dragging something." She sighed, a long, dusty sound that ended in a wheeze that made Malcolm even more nervous. "I thought if I could see what it was . . . I thought she didn't know I was following her."

"But she did."

Aggy coughed and was quiet for a moment. "She did. Up on the Fourth I heard the elevator go down. But it was a trick. She was waiting for me. I barely made it under that radiator." She flexed her tail and Malcolm now saw the long scratches in it.

Malcolm glanced down the hall. What was taking so long? Where was the Academy? But still, there was something else. "So how did the window break?"

There was a long pause and Malcolm wondered if Aggy was still with him. Finally, she creaked out, "Oh, it's been broken for ages. The lankies don't check up here often . . ."

Malcolm frowned and sat up. "No, not up here. The kindergarten room. The window was cracked."

One orange eye creaked open. "What?"

Malcolm's ears flicked. Footsteps on the stairs! The Ripe Tomato! The Academy was finally arriving. Malcolm imagined staying and explaining. But what could he say about Honey Bunny? And there would be Pete. And his extra-large and overzealous pinchers. By the time he explained, it'd be too late.

Aggy must have come to the same conclusion Malcolm had. "Malcolm," Aggy said, "you need to go. You need to stop Snip." Her voice was paper thin.

"But how will the Academy get you downstairs?"

She sighed. "It's okay, Malcolm."

A flashlight beam bobbed far down the hall in the dark. What the cheese? It wasn't the Academy—it was lankies!

At first, Malcolm's instinct was to hide, then he realized he knew exactly what to do. Kind of like how Jovahn knows how to fold together a needlenose fighter jet from a math worksheet, or how Amelia knows how to record a story. It was just there, inside of him.

Aggy needed him. The Academy wouldn't be able to move her. And they'd be too hesitant to ask for help from the lankies who could.

Malcolm stood his ground. Aggy tried to press Malcolm away with her tail. But he was stronger. He waited. The way he figured it, there was only one—well, maybe two— lankies who would likely be up here at this time of night anyway.

Hushed voices approached now.

"Tell me what it looks like again." Yes, it was Ms. Brumble.

"Well, it's a ring, so it's a thin metal circle. About the circumference of your finger." And you, Mr. Binney.

"Ha, ha." Malcolm heard the sound of you being lightly punched.

"Oh, that's not what you meant?" Malcolm could hear the smile in your voice. "Well, it was my grandmother's engagement ring. A midnight blue sapphire."

"And you've lost it."

"Well, not *lost* exactly, I'm just not sure where it is." Gristle, you were turning the wrong way! Malcolm tamped down all his ratty instincts and jumped up to dash across your beam of light, Mr. Binney.

"What was *that?*"

Malcolm stood fast in the middle of the cluttered hallway as your beam lasered in on him. "Malcolm?"

Only then did Malcolm turn back to Aggy. Your light followed him and hit Aggy's green scales. "What in the world—?"

Ms. Brumble leaned forward. "What—is that—that's the missing pet iguana!" She knelt down and touched Aggy's ruff. "Is she alive?"

You bent down. Maybe to get a closer look, maybe to scoop up Malcolm. No one knew. But Aggy didn't wait. She curled her magnificent tail protectively around Malcolm.

And she flicked.

Malcolm soared past your shoulder. You ducked and you said that word again, Mr. Binney. The swear one that

always gets Skylar in trouble. Malcolm didn't take it personally. Because he knew he'd waited long enough. He knew you would stay and do what he needed you to do. And Aggy had launched Malcolm on his way to do what he needed to do.

Malcolm sailed through the dusty air and down the hall. And when he landed (in a pile of paint drop cloths, luckily), he was off and running before you could even shine your light his way.

CHAPTER 29
A TASTE OF WATER

Malcolm spent the first minute running around in circles in the dark. Where had Snip gone? The boiler room? But Malcolm didn't even know how to get to the boiler room.

Hold on a whisker. That wasn't entirely true. There was one route he did know.

A very wet route.

Have you ever noticed that when you do something distasteful—like diving into a toilet, for example—it's not quite as disgusting if it's something you *choose* to do? Kind of like hot lunch. If you take it because you decided to sleep late and not make a lunch, that's one thing. You can live with a sausage pancake on a stick. But if you *have* to take hot lunch because you left your perfectly good peanut butter and banana sandwich on the bus and there's no way your mom can bring another to school for you because she has a meeting and she's mad at you anyway because you forgot your jacket the day before? Well, that sausage pancake on a stick is a lot harder to swallow.

I know, comparing a meal to swimming through sewers maybe isn't the best mental picture,[68] but the point is, getting flushed was one of the most humiliating things that had ever happened to Malcolm. But now?

Well, he hesitated for exactly 1.2 seconds before diving in.

Malcolm made it to the basement in record time. That little rat map system in his brain already had it all figured out. He simply had to go with the flow.

Minutes later, Malcolm peeped out of the drain in the floor of the boiler room.

He pulled himself out and shook himself dry. The room was as he remembered. The boxy metal monster roared in one corner, pulsing out air and water and who knows what else through the maze of pipes in the ceiling and walls. The room reeked of dampness, dust, and . . . decay.

And maybe more than that, too. Malcolm pressed his nose to the damp cement floor. Yes, the hand sanitizer scent was there. The chemicals. The lemon cleaning solution and the paste. He recognized the smells from upstairs. Snip was here. Malcolm trailed the scent to the clammy

---

[68] Although if you're talking about disgusting and distasteful, they *are* pretty comparable.

back corner. Here a giant tank belched and fizzed water through thick pipes.

"You're too late, you know," Snip said, and strolled out from behind the tank.

Malcolm jumped behind a tangle of pipes.

Snip laughed, a coarse, rough sound. "Oh, I'm not going to eat you. At least not right away. First, I'm going to enjoy my triumph. You know, play with my food a little."

She crouched and crawled on her belly, until her eyes were inches away and even with Malcolm's. Her tail stretched up behind her like a wiggling exclamation point. "This has been the best night of my life. First, to watch you and that silly rabbit fight. Both of you defending the school that keeps you prisoner. Both of you, afraid to trust the other one. That was delicious."

Malcolm retreated into the shadows. Those glowing eyes. That wriggling white tip of her tail! The tail did another twist and Malcolm felt himself relaxing. He tried to look away, but it was so hard. That gristly, winding, weaving tail!

"You know, Honey Bunny was right about one thing," Snip continued with a sneer. "I did need a critter to help me pull this off. And you and your rattiness were perfection. Only in a different way than he expected. While they fretted about you and how you might betray them, I was free to put my little plan into action."

What? The mention of Honey Bunny made Malcolm

close his eyes. Was Snip right? Had his rattiness caused all this to happen? What if rattiness was so deep-down strong that even if you tried to make the best choices, to be the fifth-grader you wanted to be, to be the rat you *were*, it still seeped out and ruined everything? If Malcolm hadn't convinced you to pick him as a pet and bring him to McKenna, would Amelia and Jovahn and all the other nutters, even Skylar, even *Kiera*, be safe tomorrow? Safe from whatever Snip's brew would do?

Do you believe that, Mr. Binney?

I'm guessing, but I think you don't. I think that's why you read us *Despereaux*, and why you talk to us fifth-graders about being the rats we want to be. Because I think you believe that even if you are a rat, it doesn't mean you have to be a *rat*. And especially not a rat fink.

It took Malcolm a while to get to that. After all, it's always easier to see things clearly from a distance—when you're not the one trapped alone in a musty basement at midnight by a fermented, ancient cat.

What got Malcolm there was what flashed through his ratty brain when he closed his eyes: the smell of Amelia's strawberry shampoo. The taste of Jovahn's peanut butter Ritz. The splash of Oscar helping him. The sound of Billy and Jesse saying he was a good critter. The roughness of Aggy's magnificent tail. Even the screech of Beert.

In short, all the critters and nutters who believed in him.

And it was that last one—the thought of Beert—that made Malcolm crack his eyes open.

That boarded-up window in the clock tower. It had crumbled so easily under his teeth. What if . . . Malcolm's eyes followed the pipe Snip kept gesturing toward. It led to the wall where Malcolm was hiding. It was wide, as thick as Jovahn's arm. Could he?

Malcolm scooted until he was under the pipe. He angled himself so that a vent blocked Snip's view. He scraped at the pipe with his front teeth. This wasn't like the weathered board upstairs. This was metal, heavy and thick and hard. Malcolm chipped at it. He glanced at the roaring contraption across the room. At least it drowned out the sounds he was making.

Malcolm drew back. Yes, there was a definite scratch where he had gnawed! The pipe might be metal, but it was as old as the rest of the school. Malcolm wasn't sure how this would end up for him, but maybe he could at least guarantee that Snip's brew wouldn't be in the water tomorrow.

"I don't get it," Malcolm said, trying to keep the excitement out of his voice. If he could keep Snip talking long enough . . . "Why bother?"

There was a pause. Then a long drawn-out hiss. "Why? Why? Isn't it clear? Didn't you already say? The sticky fingers and the pink ribbons! The awfulness of being a pet. The awfulness of *not* being a pet. All these years I've lived having to listen to those creatures—both in the classrooms and in the cages—laugh and team up and help one another and make friends and LEAVE ME OUT. Year after year after year. And then, last year, *she* came back." She let out a mew that was so hoarse it sounded like gravel.

Malcolm stopped gnawing. The pipe had grown warm under his teeth. "She?" Malcolm said.

Snip snapped, "Oh yes. I knew her at once. Oh, she's aged—and not well, mind you. Red hair darker. All lanky and serious now. Pushing a broom around. She uses soft hands with you pets, but she shoos me out. Out of the building I've lived in all these long years. Me, her own kitten!"

Malcolm swallowed, remembering the writing in the clock tower. "You mean Ms. Brumble, don't you? She's Veronica. And she's *your* Veronica! The girl who dressed up as a witch and left you at school on Dedication Day. Your nutter."

Snip spat. "Don't mention her name! See, that's the beauty of all this. On top of ruining that hideous tradition of Dedication Day for the creatures, she'll get some of the blame. She's the one to look after the boilers; instead, she's been mooning it up over that teacher. After all these years, I'll finally get even with the one who made me who I am." She swiped a paw under the pipe. "Where are you, rat? Enough chitchat."

Malcolm pressed his teeth harder. Then, a taste of water was under his whiskers.

240

He didn't stop. He had to make the hole bigger before Snip figured out what he was doing. Malcolm clawed and chewed. The water trickled out. It puddled on the floor under him. It spread wider and wider. Still Malcolm gnawed.

Then the wetness touched Snip's paw. She drew back. "What are you doing?" she screeched.

A huge chunk of pipe broke off in Malcolm's paws. The pipe really was very old. Water gushed out now—so fast that it pulled Malcolm off his feet. He swept past her. "What are you doing? My brew!" she cried. Then the water overtook her, too.

The water rushed across the floor, filling the nooks and crannies, getting deeper by the second. It swirled and Malcolm was swept out into the open space of the floor.

When you're an undersized rat, it doesn't take long for the water to be over your head. Malcolm rat-paddled for all he was worth. The door of the room was shut and the water pounded against it. Malcolm had loosed a flood. And it kept rising.

Malcolm was having trouble keeping his nose up. He wasn't sure if it was all he had been through, but he felt calm. And tired. He was so very tired. Tired from being out of his cage for so long. Tired from helping Beert. Tired from fighting Honey Bunny. And tired from the gnawing. But it was a good tired.

Snip leaped onto a pipe to keep from getting wet. He should tell her. He didn't think it would matter to Snip anymore, but he should say it. Malcolm took a deep breath

and called out over the sound of the water, "You should know, Snip—Blackberry. Veronica didn't forget you. She got hurt that day. Her mother said she cried more about losing you than she did about her broken ankle."

Snip climbed up to the top of the water heater. Soaking wet, Malcolm could really see her now. She was scary thin and twisted. "You—you—dirty rat. You *rat fink,*" she hissed. "You stupid, stupid rat."

"That's right," he called out, letting the current pull him toward the closed door. "That's right. I *am* a rat."

Malcolm wasn't sure Snip heard him, though. The flood

had reached the top of the water heater and now she was in the swirling mess. The space between the top of the water and cobwebby ceiling was closing fast. Malcolm knew there wasn't much time left.

Amelia, he thought. *Jovahn. Billy. Aggy. Jesse. Oscar.* His friends flashed before his eyes. He was glad he had come to McKenna. He would have never known the rat he was. Would never even have thought about it without being in your class, Mr. Binney.

Malcolm felt his body hit something hard. The water sucked and pulled at him. He struggled against the current. The door! At the top was a transom, like the doors upstairs, like the very first time he had snuck into Aggy's kindergarten room. Through that two-inch gap, the pressure of all the water in the room poured out.

An exit!

With the last ounce of his strength—rats *are* cunning survivors, you know—Malcolm took a gulp of air from the inch of space at the top of the ceiling. Then he dove down and found the transom. Malcolm felt himself being pulled with the water. Then—air!

And Malcolm was falling. Falling and landing in a growing lake on the floor in the hallway.

He inched and dragged himself down the hall. He squeezed under the first door he came across. He crawled up to safety. Up to dryness.

Everything went dark.

CHAPTER 30
THE WAY OF THE RAT

Malcolm slept like the dead. He slept so hard that he didn't hear the clock chime one o'clock, or two o'clock, or even twelve noon. He didn't even wake when Ms. Brumble opened the closet the next night and discovered him snoozing on top of her extra mop heads.

"You again!" she said, gently picking him up. "For a little guy, you sure do get around."

She carried him to the outside door. She stooped and set him on the grass. "Be good," she whispered. "Be free."

It was the smell of moonlight and wet leaves that finally woke Malcolm. He rolled over and sat up. His head buzzed. His teeth were tender. His claws stung. His tail was raw. Gristle, even his whiskers ached!

"Well, hey there," said a familiar voice from above.

Malcolm whirled around and instantly regretted the sudden movement. "Clyde!"

"Malcolm." Clyde studied him for a minute from the top of the dumpster. "You look different. You okay?"

Malcolm nodded slowly. He eased himself up. The cold of the night air seemed to be clearing his head.

"Did you see all the excitement?" Clyde asked, chomping on a curly fry.

"Excitement?"

"Yeah, yesterday. All the tall ones, buzzing around. They had all the big wheels out here. Helmeted folks parading about. Ladders up to the clock. And water everywhere. They even stopped the learning for the smaller ones and canceled school. That's why our scraps are a little low."

Wait. He had slept a whole day and into the next night? Malcolm finally stirred. That meant he had missed meeting with Amelia and Jovahn! What must they be thinking?

"Clyde," Malcolm started. "I need to go back."

"Oh, for driblets' sake! Do you have creamed corn for brains? Every time you end up out here you look worse than the last. Look at you, teeth worn to nubs. It's not healthy."

Malcolm shook his head, remembering all that had happened the night before. Yes, he had stopped Snip, he had found Aggy, but the Academy wasn't going to welcome him back. Not after Honey Bunny. And Room 11 was off-limits, too. Malcolm was still a pet who'd bitten a nutter. Even if that nutter understood. They wouldn't— couldn't—take him back. "No, it's different this time, Clyde. I'm coming back out here. Coming back to stay."

But he did have to at least let Amelia and Jovahn know he was all right. He couldn't simply disappear. "Is the window still open?" Maybe he could leave one last note.

Clyde shook his head. "No, you should see all the fussing they've been doing around here. Fixing and mending. It's like they've decided to keep all the critters in or out and stay that way."

Malcolm's disappointment must have shown on his face because Clyde continued, "But hey now. They can't keep a rat out. We've got generations, centuries, *millennia* of sneaking in where they don't want us. Let me show you a fancy way. C'mon." Clyde scampered down the side of the dumpster. He rummaged in the bushes and came out with a large serving spoon and his mouth bulging with something.

He climbed back up to the top of the dumpster. "This one's my favorite," he said, with something large in his mouth. "I invented it myself. Well, after watching a couple of the smaller ones messing around."

Malcolm watched as Clyde set the spoon across the lock of the dumpster. He spit a chalky stone from the gravel under the shrubs into the spoon before jumping on its handle. The stone sailed through the air. As it shot through the space between the dumpster and the school, it glowed in the moonlight.

Malcolm caught his breath. His body turned as cold as the night in the kindergarten room.

That stone. He had seen that stone before!

Or, at least, one like it.

Then Malcolm heard the smack of the rock hitting the window. And the splinter of glass as it shattered. Clyde yelled, "A perfect hit! Come on, Malcolm, we're in!"

Malcolm sat there, stunned. That stone. It was the same as the one inside the kindergarten room the night Aggy had disappeared. That chalky white stone he had tripped on had come from outside. From the gravel under the bushes next to the school.

It had come from Clyde.

Malcolm felt his mind fogging up. Clyde had broken Aggy's window? But why?

Clyde was already zigzagging his way up the school wall. Malcolm scampered after him. "Wait!" he called out.

"Come on," Clyde yelled from the second story. He stopped on the windowsill. "You see, they can't keep us out. We rats have the best of both worlds. The freedom of the outside; the treasures of the inside."

Malcolm caught up. His breath was ragged. He stared at Clyde. "You've done this before."

"Well, yeah. It's the way of the rat. Gotta eat," Clyde said with a grin. He took a few steps forward. "Aw, come on, what's the problem now?"

"You broke my friend's window."

Clyde frowned. "Friend? Curdled crumbs, Malcolm, you've been indoors entirely too long. They've got you talking like one of the small ones. Yes, I've been inside before. Yes, I broke a window before. But the cat was right. Lots and lots of kibble inside. And she gave me this glim! It's my best one ever." He turned and Malcolm saw something tied on Clyde's tail. A thin, round metal circle with a dazzly blue stone. Midnight blue.

Does it sound familiar, Mr. Binney? Yes, that's right: your—or rather, Ms. Brumble's—ring.

Malcolm felt like he had swallowed a whole jar of peanut butter.

"Snip gave you that? For doing what she said?"

Clyde scowled. "Well, I didn't do it because the cat said to. I did it because I wanted to. No one *tells* a rat what to do. Not a real rat, anyway," he finished pointedly. His voice hardened. "Now what's your problem with this? Aren't I showing you how to get back in?"

Malcolm felt the heat rising in him. "You broke a window and everyone thought it was me!" Suddenly, another thought hit him. "That wasn't the only time, was it? You were meeting with Snip all along. And when Honey Bunny saw you with her, he thought you were me!"

Clyde was starting to back away now. But not because

he was concerned or sorry. Malcolm could see that. Clyde was angry. "The Academy," he spit out. "Those mushy melons."

Malcolm stared. "You know the Academy?"

Clyde shrugged. "I came here as a pet, sure. Joined the Academy. Learned the ins and outs of the school. That gallumping bunny taught me. But as soon as I saw the opportunity, I was out of there. I'm much better off as an independent agent. Look, I break a window as soon as the lizard follows the cat, and all the snacks are mine. A little distraction of those pampered pets here, a little there, and

this glim around my tail. I don't know what Snip got out of it—I didn't know she was trying to make it look like it was you. I didn't even know you then!" He had reached the corner of the window ledge now. His voice turned hard. "But, by niblets, I don't care either. I got what *I* wanted. Rats are made for helping themselves, not coddling others."

Malcolm's heart pinched. If all Honey Bunny had known of rats had been Clyde—well, no wonder he thought all rats were lazy, greedy, sneaky liars, and thieves.

"But not this rat," Malcolm said softly. He straightened his spine. And then a little louder, "Not all rats are like that." He stepped toward Clyde.

Clyde looked at him in disgust. "So what're you going to do now? Go back to your friends—the ones who threw you out?"

Malcolm didn't know. But he did know he couldn't live like Clyde. And now he knew there were two things left he needed to do. A note for Amelia and Jovahn. And something for you, Mr. Binney.

In the distance, a shadow flickered in front of the moon. Malcolm acknowledged it with a nod. He pulled on the ring on Clyde's tail. "This wasn't Snip's to give away," he said. "It belongs to someone else."

Clyde growled and yanked back. He was so mad he was foaming. "You'll see. Living on your own. You'll starve. You'll see what you're willing to do then!" He shoved Malcolm, and Malcolm stumbled on the window

252

ledge. "You're nothing but a spoiled pet. You might as well be a mou—"

His words were cut off by a white swoop. A ghost dropped silently out of the sky and scooped Clyde from the windowsill with long talons. Clyde was so surprised, the ring slipped from his tail.[69] It spun through the air for a moment, its midnight blue stone dazzly glim with the moonlight. Then Malcolm—with the agility only a rat possesses—stretched out the tip of his ratty tail and neatly caught the ring.

The ghostly barn owl banked upward. He turned. And as he flew over the school with that rat fink Clyde in his talons, he nodded to Malcolm. "Perhaps *I* can help *you*," he said in his deep voice. "Know a special place for this one." Then he flew out of sight, over the oak trees.

And it was only then that a voice from inside the school spoke. A familiar voice. It said, "Perhaps you'd like to come in now. It's getting quite chilly with the window broken."

_____

[69] In truth, not nearly as magnificent as Malcolm's. Perhaps that's why Clyde disguised it with the dazzly glim.

CHAPTER 31
DWELL HERE

Malcolm was so startled by the voice, he tripped on the window ledge and fell into the room. He was on top of a bookshelf, where he tangled with a model skeleton, before crashing to the floor, the floor of the library.

A circle of critters surrounded Malcolm. But Malcolm stared at only one of them.

"Aggy," Malcolm gasped. "You're here! You're better!"

Aggy bowed her head. Her scales had gained some luster since Malcolm had last seen her. "Yes. Alive and improving, thanks to you."

Billy burst through then and flung her paws around Malcolm's neck. "Malcolm, *you're* alive. I'm so glad. *We're* so glad." Ouch! Something under Malcolm ground into his hind leg, but he was too happy to care.

Harriet the hedgehog sniffed. "We were trying to have an Academy meeting. Our first since Aggy was recovered and the school was flooded. And then you fell in." Everyone looked up at the broken window. Malcolm shifted.

And the chalky white stone rolled out from under him. The Academy all stared at it. Malcolm looked around, almost too afraid to ask. "Did you—did you all—"

"We heard, Malcolm," Jesse said. "We did. We all heard Clyde."

Tank the turtle nudged him. "We thought it was you. HB had seen a rat . . . we never knew Clyde was still around."

"Peep! Speak! Heap!" The three chicks interrupted.

Pete tucked his pincher in his shell and smiled sheepishly at the birds. "Um, perhaps you did try to tell us."

"Hey, they said a new word!" Jesse hooted. He high-fived each of them.[70]

Malcolm continued, "Clyde said he was in the Academy once."

Aggy nodded. "Clyde's is a long story, but it's why some found it so hard to trust a rat. He was Honey Bunny's pledge." She cleared her throat. "And Honey Bunny doesn't like to make mistakes."

At those words, Malcolm's throat gummed up. "I made a mistake about Honey Bunny. I thought he was the one working with Snip." He swallowed but pressed on. It was

---

[70] Well, actually high-pawed and -winged them. But you get the idea.

important to get it all out. "I was so sure it was Honey Bunny that I didn't consider anyone else."

Silence settled on the group. Then from behind Harriet, someone cleared his throat. "I think I said to not call me that."

Malcolm's eyes bugged out. How could it be? But yes, alive and scowling, with his ear bandaged and his back leg in a cast. A pink one. Honey Bunny.

"You're alive! But—but—how?"

Honey Bunny shrugged. "The tents in the courtyard."

Malcolm's mouth opened, but nothing came out. What do you say to someone you thought you had killed but then ended up not?

Honey Bunny cuffed him lightly. "Look, don't worry about it, runt. You were doing what you thought was right. No less than me. And if it weren't for you—well, who knows what Snip would have done."

The rest of the group pressed in. "Yes," said Harriet. "Aggy, we're going to reinstate, him aren't we?"

The rest of the group murmured in agreement.

Malcolm cleared his throat to interrupt. "Thank you, everyone, but please—wait. I don't want to lie anymore. No more secrets. I did talk to a nutter. Actually, two now. And I—well, I'm going to again." Malcolm pulled his tail out so that everyone could see the ring. "I need to give this back to a lanky."

Honey Bunny sighed. He hobbled closer. "Malcolm, I think we—I—gave you the wrong impression. Helping nutters and lankies is what we do. Yes, talking to them is unconventional, but I think I need to say that I've been unfair. I couldn't see beyond the fact that you are a rat." He blew out a gust of air. "I'm sorry. If you need to talk to a lanky to make things right, then we owe you that much. By claw, I'd walk you there myself, if it weren't for this busted-up leg."

Malcolm felt a warm glow growing in his chest. "Thank you, Honey—HB." He ducked his head down.

"So it's settled. You'll return to the Academy. After you return the ring," Aggy said briskly. She certainly was back to herself. "Well, do we all agree that Malcolm here shall be considered a full member? I think his pledge time is more than over."

Malcolm looked from critter face to critter face. Harriet sniffed but didn't say anything.

But something was still bothering Malcolm. Yes, he wanted to be back with the Academy, with McKenna School, with the nutters, but maybe the critters didn't know—"Aggy? I'd love to join you, but I can't go back to Room Eleven. I bit a nutter."

From the front desk, a splashing noise started up. "Oscar!" Billy cried. She darted up to the aquarium, where Oscar shifted and rearranged the beads and letters. Billy read aloud, "WELCOME BACK NOT A RAT. R FOUR TWENTY-THREE."[71]

---

[71] The exact number has been changed to protect the privacy of the Academy. You understand, right, Mr. Binney?

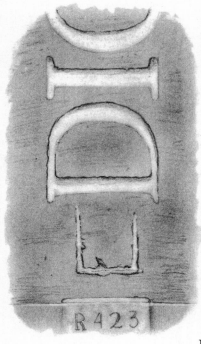

"R four twenty-three?" Jesse repeated. Octavius shrugged.

But Malcolm knew what Oscar meant. He moved to the bookshelves. "R four twenty-three." Malcolm stopped in front of a giant dictionary on a bottom shelf. It was as big as six social studies textbooks stacked together. It was almost as big as Malcolm's super-deluxe cage back in Room 11.

Malcolm sniffed it. He pawed at it. And then he saw it. On the spine of the book. A Mark.

The Midnight Academy had followed Malcolm to the book. Aggy sucked in her breath. "That's an old one. We don't even use it anymore. It means 'dwell here.'" She looked around at the group and everyone shook their heads. How long had this been Marked? Why? Who else had lived there?

Malcolm squeezed around to the back of the shelf. And found that the book was hollowed out. He *could* dwell here. He could stay snug as a . . . well, a rat in a really big dictionary. And by night? He'd come out to serve the Academy.

Aggy said, "Octavius? We'll need to record all this. Malcolm, you weren't in the Academy long enough to know, but we keep minutes of all adventures and transactions. You'll need to start meeting with Octavius."

Malcolm poked his head out from his new dictionary dwelling. It had given him an idea. "Um, Aggy? What if—would it be okay—well, Amelia—my nutter—she and I kind of have a system. And she's a really fast typist. Maybe if I told the story to her, she could write it down?"

The other critters fell silent.

It was Honey Bunny who spoke up. "I think that's a grand idea. That frees up Octavius here. Because we still have a lot of loose ends to wrap up. There's been no sign of Snip since yesterday night, but we're not sure what that means. And I'd like to talk to that owl—from a respectable distance, mind you—to see what he did with that scoundrel Clyde. Maybe he'd like to join us. We could use some reconnaissance on the outside . . ."

Honey Bunny blathered on, but Malcolm's ears drooped. Gristle, he was tired again. And the Niche was so cozy. Someone had filled it with rags. They didn't smell quite as nice as Amelia's strawberry shampoo, but they'd do. Malcolm wiggled in. The murmur of the Academy filled the room as Malcolm folded his ears down and pulled his tail around him. The ring was still there. It'd be okay for a while longer. A nap, then Malcolm would put the ring on your desk, Mr. Binney. And then maybe a snack. Malcolm wondered if Jesse or Billy would be up for a Nosh and Fodder later on. Or maybe he'd take them down to play in the boiler room.

But before he could even ask, Malcolm drifted off to sleep.

And we all know what that meant.

Being the rat you are—a rat of valor and merit—is really very exhausting.

Or maybe it meant that Malcolm the Rat was finally, finally home.

EPILOGUE, OR, THOUGHT YOU MIGHT WANT TO KNOW

Dear Readers,

It should be noted that this story—Malcolm's story—isn't completely done, even though the writers have finished writing it. No, there's one last part you should know about.

One day in winter, not long after Mr. Binney read Malcolm's story, the fifth-graders of Room 11 came into the classroom to find their teacher sitting on his stool as usual at the front of the room. On one side of him sat Ms. Brumble.[72] On the other side was Malcolm's old three-story cage—with the

---

[72] With a dazzly midnight blue ring on her finger.

drip-free antibacterial water bottle, fleece-lined Comf-E-Cube, tail-safe wheel, and all.

Mr. Binney grinned. "Come on in, everybody. I'd like to introduce you to our new classroom pet." He reached his hand in the cage, scooped out a critter, and placed him on his shoulder. "Malcolm. Meet Malcolm the Rat."

"But Mr. Binney, that's the same mou—"

Mr. Binney carefully cleared his throat. "No, Kiera," he said firmly. "Can't you tell? This is clearly a rat. Not a mouse. Look at his magnificent tail. His whiskers. His intelligent coffee-black eyes. Clearly a rat. A rat of some valor and merit, in fact. Right, Amelia? Jovahn?"

Amelia and Jovahn, who were sitting next to each other, grinned back. "Right," said Amelia.

"But—" Kiera started.

Jovahn elbowed her gently. "He's definitely a rat, Kiera."

"Furthermore, I have a new read-aloud for us," Mr. Binney said, moving on. (Mr. Binney had learned in all his years of teaching that sometimes what works best with students like Kiera is to Just Keep Going.)

The class drew up their chairs. It wasn't really read-aloud time—first thing in the morning. But no one was going to argue with Mr. Binney. Ever since the morning he had found that ring on his desk, he had been different. And any numb-brain would take read-aloud over the usual daily math warm-up.

"Today," said Mr. Binney, "I'm going to read to you one

of my favorite stories." He reached behind him and pulled out a stack of papers. "It's a story about a rat hero. It's called *Malcolm at Midnight*."

And that, Readers, is the *real* end of the story. Thought you might want to know. It turns out that a lot happens in a school even if the teachers *are* looking.

Sincerely,

Mr. Mark Binney, fifth grade teacher

ACKNOWLEDGMENTS

I Know (with a capital K) that Malcolm would not be who he is without the support and input from a long list of people: My early listener, Cal. My very patient sounding boards, Don and Eli. My writer-readers, Kami Kinard, Kathryn Erskine, and Kristen Kittscher. The SCBWI for a work-in-progress grant encouraging me to finish my silly footnoted talking animal mystery. Linda Pratt, for finding Malcolm such a happy home. Brian Lies, for his questions as well as his art. And finally, everyone at Houghton Mifflin Books for Children, especially Kate O'Sullivan, Scott Magoon, Rachel Wasdkye, and Jennifer LaBracio. Crumb, you guys are good.